A CHRISTMAS GUEST

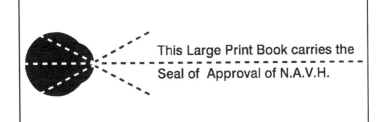

This Large Print Book carries the
Seal of Approval of N.A.V.H.

A CHRISTMAS GUEST

ANNE PERRY

THORNDIKE PRESS

An imprint of Thomson Gale, a part of The Thomson Corporation

THOMSON
━━━━━━✦━━━━━━ TM
GALE

Detroit • New York • San Francisco • New Haven, Conn. • Waterville, Maine • London • Munich

LIBRARY OF CONGRESS CATALOGING-IN-PUBLICATION DATA

Perry, Anne.
    A Christmas guest / by Anne Perry.
        p. cm. "Thorndike Press large print basic" — T.p. verso.
    ISBN 0-7862-8816-7 (hardcover : alk. paper)
    1. Women detectives — France — Loire River Valley — Fiction. 2. Loire River Valley (France) — Fiction. 3. British — France — Fiction. 4. Grandmothers — Fiction. 5. Large type books. 6. Christmas stories. I. Title.
PR6066.E693C468 2006
823'.914—dc22   2006016544

Published in 2006 by arrangement with The Ballantine Publishing Group, a division of Random House, Inc.

Printed in the United States of America on permanent paper
10 9 8 7 6 5 4 3 2 1

To all those who are still
hoping and still learning

■ ■ ■ ■

PART ONE

■ ■ ■ ■

"I do not accept it!" Mariah Ellison said indignantly. It was intolerable.

"I am afraid there is no alternative," Emily replied. She was wearing a beautiful morning dress of pale water green with fashionably large sleeves and a sweeping skirt. With her fair coloring, it made her look prettier than she was, and having married money she had airs above her station.

"Of course there is an alternative!" Grandmama snapped, staring up at her from her chair in the withdrawing room. "There is always an alternative. Why in heaven's name should you wish to go to France? It is only a week and a half until Christmas!"

Emily sighed deeply. "We have been invited to spend Christmas in the Loire valley."

"*Where* in France is immaterial. It is still not England. We shall have to cross the

Channel. It will be rough and we shall all be ill."

"I know it would be unpleasant for you," Emily conceded. "And the train journey from Paris might be tedious, and perhaps cold at this time of year . . ."

"What do you mean *perhaps?*" Grandmama snapped. "There is no possible doubt."

"So perhaps it is as well that you were not invited." Emily gave a very slight smile. "Now you will not have to worry how to decline with grace."

Grandmama had a sharp suspicion that Emily was being sarcastic. She also had an unpleasant and surprisingly painful realization. "Do I take it that you are going to leave me alone in this house for Christmas while you go visiting wherever you said it was, in France?" She tried to keep her voice angry rather than betraying her sudden sense of being abandoned.

"Of course not, Grandmama," Emily said cheerfully. "It would be quite miserable for you. But apart from that, you can't stay here because there will be nobody to care for you."

"Don't be absurd!" Grandmama regained her temper with asperity. "There is a houseful of servants." Emily's Christmas parties were among the few things Grandmama had been looking forward to, although she would have choked rather than admit it. She would have attended as though it were a duty required of her, and then loved every moment. "You have sufficient housemaids for a duchess! I have never seen so many girls with mops and dusters in my life!"

"The servants are coming with us and you cannot stay here alone at Christmas. It would be wretched. I have made arrangements for you to go and stay with Mama and Joshua."

"I have no desire to stay with your mother and Joshua," Grandmama said instantly.

Caroline had been her daughter-in-law, until Edward's death a few years ago had left her a widow of what Grandmama referred to as "an unfortunate age." Instead of settling into a decent retirement from society, as the dear Queen had done, and as everyone had expected of her, Caroline had married again. That in itself was indiscreet enough, but instead of a widower with means and position, which might have had considerable advantages and been looked upon with approval, she had married a man nearly two decades younger than herself. But worse than that, if anything could be, he was on the boards — an actor! A grown man who dressed up and strutted around on the stage, pretending to be someone else. And he was Jewish, for heaven's sake!

Caroline had lost what wits she had ever had, and poor Edward would be turning in his grave, if he knew. It was one of the many burdens of Grandmama's life that she had lived long enough to see it. "No desire at all," she repeated.

Emily stood quite still in the middle of the withdrawing room, the firelight casting a warm glow on her skin and the extravagant coils of her hair. "I'm sorry, Grandmama, but as I said, there really is no choice," she repeated. "Jack and I are leaving tomorrow, and there is a great deal of packing to do, as we shall be gone for at least three weeks. You had best take a good supply of warmer gowns, and boots, and you may borrow my black shawl if you would care to?"

"Good gracious! Can they not afford a fire?" Grandmama said furiously. "Perhaps Joshua should consider a more respectable form of employment? If there is anything else on earth he is fitted for?"

"It has nothing to do with money," Emily retorted. "They are spending Christmas in a house on the south coast of Kent. The Romney Marshes, to be exact. I daresay the wind will be chill, and one often feels the cold more when away from home."

Grandmama was appalled! In fact she was so appalled it was several seconds before she could find any words at all to express her horror. "I think I misheard you," she said icily at last. "You mumble these days. Your diction used to be excellent, but since your marriage to Jack Radley you have allowed your standards to slip . . . in several areas. I thought you said that your mother is going to spend Christmas in some bog by the sea. As that is obviously complete nonsense, you had better repeat yourself, and speak properly."

"They have taken a house in Romney Marsh," Emily said with deliberate clarity. "It is near the sea, and I believe the views will be very fine, if there is no fog, of course."

Grandmama looked for impertinence in Emily's face, and saw an innocence so wide-eyed as to be highly suspicious.

"It is unacceptable," she said in a tone that would have frozen water in a glass.

Emily stared at her for a moment, regathering her thoughts. "There is too much wind at this time of the year for there to be much fog," she said at last. "Perhaps you can watch the waves?"

"In a marsh?" Grandmama asked sarcastically.

"The house is actually in St. Mary in the Marsh," Emily replied. "It is very close to the sea. It will be pleasant. You don't have to go outside if it is cold and you don't wish to."

"Of course it will be cold! It is on the English Channel, in the middle of winter. I shall probably catch my death."

To give her credit, Emily did look a little uncomfortable. "No you won't," she said with forced cheer. "Mama and Joshua will look after you very well. You might even meet some interesting people."

"Stuff and nonsense!" Grandmama said furiously.

Nevertheless the old lady had no choice, and the next day she found herself sitting with her maid, Tilly, in Emily's carriage. It made slow progress out of the city traffic, then sped up as it reached the open road south of the river and proceeded toward Dover, roughly a hundred and forty-five miles southeast of London.

Of course she had known the journey would be dreadful. To make it in one day she had set out before dawn, and it would be late before they reached whatever god-

14

forsaken spot in which Caroline had chosen to spend Christmas. Heaven alone knew what it would be like! If they were in trying circumstances it might be no more than a cottage without civilized facilities, and so cramped she would spend the entire time forced into their company. It was going to be the worst Christmas of her life!

Emily's thoughtlessness in gallivanting off to France, of all places, at this time of year, was beyond belief! It was an outrage against all family loyalty and duty.

The day was gray and still, and mercifully the rain was no more than a spattering now and then. They stopped for luncheon, and to change the horses, and again a little after four o'clock for afternoon tea. By that time, naturally, it was dark and she had not the faintest idea where she was. She was tired, her legs were cramped from the long sitting, and unavoidably she was rattled and jolted around with the constant movement. And of course it was cold — perishingly so.

They stopped again to inquire the way as lanes grew narrower and even more rutted and overhung. When at last they arrived at their destination she was in a temper fit to have lit a fire with the sheer heat of her words. She climbed out with the coachman's assistance, and stood on the gravel drive of what was obviously a fairly large house. All the lights seemed to be blazing and the front door was decorated with a magnificent wreath of holly.

Immediately she was aware of the smells of smoke and salt, and a sharp wind with an edge to it like a slap in the face. It was damp, so no doubt it was straight off the sea. Caroline had obviously lost not only her money but the last vestige of her senses as well.

The door opened and Caroline came down the steps now, smiling. She was still a remarkably handsome woman in her fifties, her dark mahogany hair only lightly sprinkled with the odd silver at the temples, which had a softening effect. She was dressed in deep, warm red and it gave a glow to her skin.

"Welcome to St. Mary, Mama-in-law," she said a trifle guardedly.

The old lady could think of nothing whatever that met the situation, or her feelings. She was tired, confused, and utterly miserable in a strange place where she knew perfectly well she was unwanted.

It was several months since she had seen her erstwhile daughter-in-law. They had never been genuinely friends, although they had lived in the same house for over twenty years. During her son Edward's lifetime there had been a truce. Afterward Caroline had behaved disgracefully and would listen to no advice at all. It became necessary for Grandmama to find other accommodations because Caroline and Joshua moved around so much, as his ridiculous profession dictated. There was never a question of Grandmama living with Charlotte, the elder granddaughter. She had scandalized everyone by marrying a policeman, a man of no breeding, no money, and an occupation that defied polite description. Heaven only knew how they survived!

So she had had no choice but to live with Emily, who at least had inherited very considerable means from her first husband.

"Come in and warm yourself." Caroline offered her arm. Grandmama briskly declined it, leaning heavily on her stick instead. "Would you like a cup of tea, or hot cocoa?" Caroline continued.

Grandmama would, and said so, stepping inside to a spacious and well-lit hall. It was a trifle low-ceilinged perhaps, but floored with excellent parquet. The stairs swept up to a landing above and presumably several bedrooms. If the fires were kept stoked and the cook were any good, it might be endurable after all.

The footman carried her cases in and Tilly followed behind him. Joshua came forward and welcomed her, taking her cape himself. She was escorted into the withdrawing room where there was a blazing fire in a hearth large enough to have accommodated half a tree.

"Perhaps you would enjoy a glass of sherry after such a long journey?" Joshua offered. He was a slender man of little above average height, but possessed of extraordinary grace, and the suppleness and beauty of an actor's voice. He was not handsome in a traditional sense — his nose was rather too prominent, his features too mobile — but he had a presence one could not ignore. Every prejudice in her dictated that she dislike him, yet he had sensed her feelings far more accurately than Caroline had.

"Thank you," she accepted. "I would."

He poured a full glass from the crystal decanter and brought it to her. They sat and made conversation about the area, its features, and a little of its history. After half an hour she retired to bed, surprised to find it was still only quarter past ten, a perfectly reasonable hour. She had imagined it to be the middle of the night. It felt like it, and it was irritating to be wrong.

■ ■ ■ ■

She awoke in the morning after having slept all night almost without moving. From the amount of light coming through the curtains it appeared to be quite late, possibly even after breakfast. She had barely bothered to look at her surroundings when she arrived. Now she saw that it was an agreeable room if a trifle old-fashioned, which normally she approved of. The modern style of having less furniture, making far too much open space — no tassels, frills, carvings, embroidered samplers, and photographs on the walls and on every available surface — she found too sparse. It made a place look as if no one lived there, or if they did, then they had no family or background they dared to display.

But here she was determined not to like anything. She had been put upon, dismissed from such home as she had, and packed off to the seaside like a maid who had got herself with child, and needed to be removed until it all could be dealt with. It was a cruel and irresponsible way to treat one's grandmother. But then all respect had disappeared in modern times. The young had no manners left at all.

She rose and dressed, with Tilly's assistance, then went downstairs, more than ready for something to eat.

Then she found to her fury that Caroline and Joshua had risen early and gone for a walk toward the beach. She was obliged to have toast and marmalade and a lightly boiled egg, sitting by herself in the dining room at one end of a finely polished mahogany table surrounded by fourteen chairs. It was agreeably warm in the house, and yet she felt cold, not of the body so much as of the mind. She did not belong here. She was acquainted with no one. Even the servants were strangers about whom she knew nothing at all, nor they of her. There was nothing to do and no one to talk to.

When she had finished she stood up and went to the long windows. It looked bitterly cold outside: a wind-ragged sky, clouds torn apart and streaming across a bleached blue as if the color had died in it. The trees were leafless; black branches wet and shivering, bending at the tops. There was nothing in the garden that looked even remotely like a flower. An old man walked along the lane beyond the gate, his hat jammed on his head, scarf ends whipped around his shoulders and flapping behind him. He did not even glance in her direction.

She went into the withdrawing room where the fire was roaring comfortably, and sat down to wait for Caroline and Joshua to return. She was going to be bored to weeping, and there was no help for it. It was a bitter thing to be so abandoned in her old age.

Might there be any sort of social life at all in this godforsaken spot? She rang the bell and in a few moments the maid appeared, a country girl by the look of her.

"Yes, Mrs. Ellison?" she said expectantly.

"What is your name?" Grandmama demanded.

"Abigail, ma'am."

"Perhaps you can tell me, Abigail, what people do here, other than attend church? I presume there is a church?"

"Yes, ma'am. St. Mary the Virgin."

"What else? Are there societies, parties? Do people hold musical evenings, or lectures? Or anything at all?"

The girl looked dumbfounded. "I don't know, ma'am. I'll ask Cook." And before Grandmama could excuse her, she turned and fled.

"Fool!" Grandmama said under her breath. Where on earth was Caroline? How long would she walk in a howling gale? She was besotted with Joshua and behaving like a girl. It was ridiculous.

It turned out to be another hour and a half before they came in cheerful, wind-blown, and full of news about all kinds of local events that sounded provincial and desperately boring. Some old gentleman was going to speak about butterflies at the local church hall. A maiden lady intended to discuss her travels in an unknown area of Scotland, or worse than that, one that had been known and forgotten — doubtless for very good reasons.

"Does anyone play cards?" Grandmama inquired. "Other than Snap, or Old Maid?"

"I have no idea," Caroline replied, moving closer to the fire. "I don't play, so I have never asked."

"It requires intelligence and concentration," Grandmama told her waspishly.

"And a great deal of time on your hands," Caroline added. "And nothing better to fill it with."

"It is better than gossiping about your neighbors," Grandmama rejoined. "Or licking your lips over other people's misfortunes!"

Caroline gave her a chilly look, and controlled her temper with an effort the old lady could easily read in her face. "We shall be having luncheon at one," she observed.

"If you care to take a walk, it's wintry, but quite pleasant. And it might rain tomorrow."

"Of course it might rain tomorrow," Grandmama said tartly. "In a climate like ours that is hardly a perspicacious remark. It might rain tomorrow, any day of the year!"

Caroline did not try to mask the irritation she felt, or the effort it cost her not to retaliate. The fact that she had to try so hard gave the old lady a small, perverse satisfaction. Good! At least she still had some semblance of moral duty left! After all, she had been Edward Ellison's wife most of her adult life! She owed Mariah Ellison something!

"Maybe I shall go for a walk this afternoon," she said. "That maid mentioned something about a church, I believe."

"St. Mary the Virgin," Caroline told her. "Yes, it's attractive. Norman to begin with. The soil is very soft here so the tower has huge buttresses supporting it."

"We are on a marsh," Grandmama sniffed. "Probably everything is sinking. It is a miracle we are not up to our knees in mud, or worse!"

And so it passed for most of the next two long-drawn-out days. Walking in the garden was miserable; almost everything had died back into the earth, the trees were leafless and black and seemed to drip incessantly. It was too late even for the last roses, and too early for the first snowdrops.

There was nothing worth doing, no one to speak to or visit. Those who did call were excruciatingly boring. They had nothing to talk about except people Grandmama did not know, or wish to. They had never been to London and knew nothing of fashion, society, or even current events of any importance in the world.

Then in the middle of the second afternoon a letter arrived for Joshua. He tore it open as they were having tea in the withdrawing room, the fire roaring halfway up the chimney, rain beating on the window in the dark as heavy clouds obscured even the shreds of winter light. There was hot tea on a silver tray and toasted crumpets with butter melted into them and golden syrup on top. Cook had made a particularly good Madeira cake and drop scones accompanied by butter, raspberry jam, and cream so thick one could have eaten it with a fork.

"It's a letter from Aunt Bedelia," Joshua said, looking at Caroline, a frown on his face. "She says Aunt Maude has returned without any warning, from the Middle East, and expects them to put her up for Christmas. But it's quite impossible. They have another guest of great importance whom they cannot turn out to make room for her."

"But it's Christmas!" Caroline said with dismay. "Surely they can make room somehow? They can't turn her away. She's family. Have they a very small house? Perhaps a neighbor would accommodate her, at least overnight?"

Joshua's face tightened. He looked troubled and a little embarrassed. "No, their house is large, at least five or six bedrooms."

"If they have plenty of room, then what is this about?" Caroline asked, an edge to her voice, as if she feared the answer.

Joshua lowered his eyes. "I don't know. I called her Aunt Bedelia, but actually she is my mother's cousin and I never knew her very well, or her sister Agnes. And Maude left England about the time I was born."

"Left England?" Caroline was astounded. "You mean permanently?"

"Yes, I believe so."

"Why?"

Joshua colored unhappily. "I don't know. No one will say."

"It sounds as if they simply don't want her there," Grandmama said candidly. "As an excuse it is tissue-thin. What on earth do they expect you to do?"

Joshua looked straight at her and his eyes made her feel uncomfortable, although she had no idea why. He had fine eyes, a dark hazel-brown and very direct.

"Mama-in-law," he replied, using a title for her to which he had no right at all. "They are sending her here."

"That's preposterous!" Grandmama said more loudly than she had intended. "What can you do about it?"

"Make her welcome," he replied. "It will not be difficult. We have two other bed-rooms."

Caroline hesitated only a moment. "Of course," she agreed, smiling. "There is plenty of everything. It will be no trouble at all."

Grandmama could hardly believe it! They were going to have this wretched woman here! As if being banished herself, like secondhand furniture, were not bad enough, now she would have to divide what little attention or courtesy she received with some miserable woman, whose own family could not endure her. They would have to cater to her needs and no doubt listen to endless, pointless stories of whatever benighted spot she had been in. It was all really far too much.

"I have a headache," she announced, and

rose to her feet. "I shall go and lie down in my room." She stumped over to the door, deliberately leaning heavily on her stick, which actually she did not require.

"Good idea," Caroline agreed tartly. "Dinner will be at eight."

Grandmama could not immediately make up her mind whether to be an hour early, or fifteen minutes late. Perhaps early would be better. If she were late they were just rude enough to start without her, and she would miss the soup.

Maude Barrington arrived the following morning, alighting without assistance from the carriage that had brought her and walking with an easy step up to the front door where Joshua and Caroline were waiting for her. Grandmama had chosen to watch from the withdrawing room window, where she had an excellent view without either seeming inquisitive, which was so vulgar, or having to pretend to be pleased and welcoming, which would be farcical. She was furious.

Maude was quite tall and unbecomingly square-shouldered. A gentle curve would have been better, more feminine. Her hair appeared to be of no particular color but at least there was plenty of it. At the moment far too much poked out from underneath a hat that might have been fashionable once, but was now a disaster. She wore a traveling costume that looked as if it had been traipsed around most of the world, especially the hot and dusty parts, and now had no distinguishable shape or color left.

Maude herself could never have been pretty — her features were too strong. Her mouth in particular was anything but dainty. It was impossible to judge accurately how old she was, other than between fifty and sixty. Her stride was that of a young woman — or perhaps a young man would have been more accurate. Her skin was appalling! Either no one had ever told her not to sit in the sun, or she had totally ignored them. It was positively weather-beaten, burned, and a most unfortunate shade of ruddy brown. Heaven only knew where she had been! She looked like a native! No wonder her family did not want her there at Christmas. They might wish to entertain guests, and they could hardly lock her away.

But it was monstrous that they should wish her on Joshua and Caroline, not to mention their guests!

She heard voices in the hallway, and then footsteps up the stairs. No doubt at luncheon she would meet this miserable woman and have to be civil to her.

And so it turned out. One would have expected in the circumstances that the wretched creature would have remained silent, and spoken only when invited to do so. On the contrary, she engaged in conversation in answer to the merest question, and where a word or two would have been quite sufficient.

"I understand you have just returned from abroad," Caroline said courteously. "I hope it was pleasant?" She left it open for an easy dismissal if it were not a subject Maude wished to discuss.

But apparently it was. A broad smile lit Maude's face, bringing life to her eyes, even passion. "It was marvelous!" she said, her voice vibrant. "The world is more terrible and beautiful than we can possibly imagine, or believe, even after one has seen great stretches of it. There are always new shocks and new miracles around each corner."

"Were you away long?" Caroline asked, apparently forgetting what Joshua had told her. Perhaps she did not wish to appear to Maude as if they had been discussing her.

Maude smiled, showing excellent teeth, even though her mouth was much too big. "Forty years," she replied. "I fell in love."

Caroline clearly did not know what to make of that. Maude's hands were innocent of rings and she had introduced herself by her maiden name. The only decent thing to do would have been to avoid the subject, but she had made that impossible. No wonder they had found it intolerable to have her at home. Really, this imposition was too much!

Maude glanced at Grandmama, and cannot have failed to see the disapproval in her face. "In love with the desert," she explained lightly. "And cities like Marrakech. Have you ever been to a Muslim city in Africa, Mrs. Ellison?"

Grandmama was outraged.

"Certainly not!" she snapped. The question was ridiculous. What decent English-woman would do such a thing?

Maude was not to be stopped. She leaned forward over the table, soup forgotten. "It is flat, an oasis facing the Atlas Mountains, and stretches out from the great red tower of the Koutoubya to the blue-palmed fringes and the sands beyond. The Almoravid princes who founded it came with their hordes from the black desert of Senegal, and built palaces of beauty to rival anything on earth."

Caroline and Joshua forgot their soup also, though Grandmama did not.

"They imported masters of chiseled plaster, gilded cedar, and ceramic mosaics," Maude continued. "They created garden beyond garden, courts that led to the other courts and apartments, some high in the sunlight, others deep within walls and shadows and running water." She smiled at some inner delight. "One can walk in the green gloom of a cypress garden. Or breathe in the cool sweetness of a tunnel of jasmine where the light is soft and ever whispering with the sound of water and the murmur of pigeons as they preen themselves. There are alabaster urns, light through jeweled glass, and vermilion doors painted with arabesques in gold." She stopped for a moment to draw breath.

Grandmama felt excluded from this magic that Maude had seen, and from the table where Joshua and Caroline hung on every word. She was totally unnecessary here. She wanted to dismiss it all as foreign, and completely vulgar, but deeply against her will she was fascinated. Naturally she would not dream of saying so.

"And you were allowed to see all these

things?" Caroline said in amazement.

"I lived there, for a while," Maude answered, her eyes bright with memory. "It was a superb time, something marvelous or terrible every week. I have never been more intensely alive! The world is so beautiful sometimes I felt as if I could hardly bear it. One gazes at things that hurt with the passion of their loveliness." She smiled but her eyes were misted with tears. "Dusk in a Persian garden, the sun's fire dying on the mountains in purple and umber and rose; the call of the little owls in the coolness of the night; dimpled water over old stones; the perfume of jasmine in the moonlight, rich as sweet oil and clear as the stars; firelight reflected on a copper drum."

She pushed her soup away, too filled with emotion to eat. "I could go on forever. I cannot imagine boredom. Surely it is worse than dying, like some terrible, corroding illness that leaves you neither the joy and the hunger of life nor the release of death. Even that exquisite squeezing of the heart because you cannot hold the light forever is better than not to have seen it or loved it at all."

Grandmama had no idea what on earth she was babbling about! Of course she hadn't. At least not more than a needle-sharp suspicion, like a wound too deep to feel at first, narrow as a blade of envy, cutting almost without awareness.

What would anyone reply to such a thing? There ought to be something, but what was there that met such a . . . a baring of emotion? It was unseemly, like taking off one's clothes in public. No taste at all. That was what came of traveling to foreign parts, and not only foreign but heathen as well. It would be best to ignore the whole episode.

But of course that was quite impossible. The afternoon was cold but quite clear and sunny, although the wind was sharp. Escape was the only solution.

"I shall go for a walk," she announced after luncheon was over. "Perhaps a breath of sea air would be pleasant."

"What an excellent idea," Maude said with enthusiasm. "It is a perfect day. Do you mind if I come with you?"

What could she say? She could hardly refuse. "I'm afraid there will be no jasmine flowers or owls, or sunset over the desert," she replied coolly. "And I daresay you will find it very chilly . . . and . . . ordinary."

A shadow crossed Maude's face, but whether it was the thought of the lonely marsh and sea wind, or the rejection implicit in Grandmama's reply, it was impossible to say.

Grandmama felt a jab of guilt. The woman had been refused the comfort or sanctuary of her own home. She deserved at least civility. "But of course you are welcome to come," she added grudgingly. Blast the woman for putting her in a position where she had to say that.

Maude smiled. "Thank you."

They set out together, well wrapped up with capes and shawls, and of course strong winter boots. Grandmama closed the gate and immediately turned to the lane toward the sea. In the summer it would be overhung with may blossom and the hedgerows deep with flowers. Now it was merely sparse and wet. If the wind were cold enough, after all her living in the desert and such places, the very damp of it alone should be sufficient to make Maude tire of the idea within half an hour at the most.

But Maude was indecently healthy and used to walking. It took Grandmama all her breath and strength to keep up with her. It was roughly a mile to the seashore itself and Maude did not hesitate in her stride even once. She seemed to take it for granted that the old lady would have no difficulty in keeping up, which was extremely irritating and quite thoughtless of her. Grandmama was at least fifteen years older, if not more, and of course she was a lady, not some creature who gallivanted all over the world and went around on her feet as if she had no carriage to her name.

The sky above them was wide and wild, an aching void of blue with just a few clouds like mares' tails shredded across the east on the horizon above the sea. Gulls, dazzling white in the winter sun, wheeled and soared in the air, letting out their shrill cries like noisy children. The wind rippled the grass, flowerless, and everything smelled of salt.

"This is wonderful!" Maude said happily. "I have never smelled anything so clean and so madly alive. It is as if the whole world were full of laughter. It is so good to be back in England. I forgot how the spirit of the land is still so untamed, in spite of all we've done. I was in Snave so short a time I had no chance to get out of the house!"

She is not sane, Grandmama thought to herself grimly. No wonder her family wants to get rid of her!

They breasted the rise and the whole panorama of the English Channel opened up before them, the long stretch of sand, wind, and water bleached till it gleamed bone pale in the light. The surf broke in ranks of white waves, hissing up the shore, foaming like lace, consuming themselves, and rushing back again. Then a moment later they roared in inches higher, never tired of the game. The surface was cold, unshadowed blue, and it stretched out endlessly till it met the sky. They both knew that France was not much more than twenty miles away, but today the horizon was smudged and softened with mist that blurred the line.

Maude stood with her head high, wind unraveling the last of her hair from its pins and all but taking her shawl as well.

"Isn't it glorious?" she asked. "Until this moment I had forgotten just how much I love the sea, its width, its shining, endless possibilities. It's never the same two moments together."

"It always looks the same to me," Grandmama said ungraciously. How could anyone be so pointlessly joyous? It was half-witted! "Cold, wet, and only too happy to drown you if you are foolish enough to give it the chance," she finished.

Maude burst into laughter. She stood on the shore with her eyes closed, her face lifted upward, smiling, and the wind billowing her shawl and her skirts.

Grandmama swiveled around and stamped back onto the tussock grass, or whatever it was that tangled her feet, and started back along the lane. The woman was as mad as a hatter. It was unendurable that anyone should be expected to put up with her.

The following day was no better. Maude usurped every moment by regaling them with tales of boating on the Nile, buffalo standing in the water, unnameable insects, and tombs of kings who worshipped animals! All very fashionable, perhaps, but disgusting. Both Caroline and Joshua took hospitality too far, and pretended to be absorbed in it, even encouraging her by asking questions.

Of course the wretched woman obliged, particularly at the dinner table. And all through the roast beef, the Yorkshire pudding and the vegetables, followed by apple charlotte and cream, her captive audience were made to listen to descriptions of ruined gardens in Persia.

"I stood there in the sand of the stream splashing its way over the blue tiles, most of them broken," Maude said, smiling as her eyes misted with memory. "We were quite high up and I looked through the old trees toward the flat, brown plain, and saw those roads: to the east toward Samarkand, to the west to Baghdad, and to the south to Isfahan, and my imagination soared into flight. The very names are like an incantation. As dusk drew around me and the pale colors deepened to gold and fire and that strange richness of porphyry, in my mind I could hear the camel bells and see that odd, lurching gait of theirs as they moved silently like dreams through the coming night, bound on adventures of the soul."

"Isn't it hard sometimes?" Caroline asked, not in criticism but perhaps even sympathy.

"Oh yes! Often," Maude agreed. "You are thirsty, your body aches, and of course you can become so tired you would sell everything you possess for a good night's sleep. But you know it will be worth it. And it always is. The pain is only for a moment, the joy is forever."

And so it went on. Now and then she picked at the macadamia nuts she had brought to the table to share, saying that her family had given them to her, knowing her weakness for them.

Only Joshua accepted.

"Indigestible," Grandmama said, growing more and more irritated by it all.

"I know," Maude agreed. "I daresay I shall be sorry tonight. But a little peppermint water will help."

"I prefer not to be so foolish in the first

place," Grandmama said icily.

"Do you have peppermint water?" Caroline asked. "I can give you some, if you wish?"

"I prefer to exercise a little self-control in the first place," Grandmama answered, as if the offer had been addressed to her.

Maude smiled. "Thank you, but I have one dose, and I'm sure that will be sufficient. There are not so many nuts, and I can't resist them."

She offered the dish to Joshua again and he took two more, and asked her to continue with her tales of Persia.

Grandmama tried to ignore it.

It seemed as if morning, noon, and night they were obliged to talk about or listen to accounts of some alien place, and pretend to be interested. She had been right in the very beginning: This was going to be the worst Christmas of her life. She would never forgive Emily for banishing her here. It was a monstrous thing to have done.

She awoke in the morning to hear one of the maids screeching and banging on the door. Was there no end to the lack of consideration in this house? She sat upright in bed just as the stupid girl burst through into the room, face ashen white, mouth wide open, and eyes like holes in her head.

"Pull yourself together, girl!" Grandmama snapped at her. "What on earth is the matter with you? Stand up straight and stop sniveling. Explain yourself!"

The girl made a masterful attempt, took a gulping breath, and spoke in between gasps. "Please ma'am, somethin' terrible 'as 'appened. Miss Barrington's stone cold dead in 'er bed, she is."

"Nonsense!" Grandmama replied. "She was perfectly all right at dinner yesterday evening. She's probably just very deeply asleep."

"No, ma'am, she in't. I knows dead when I sees it, an' when I touches it. Dead as a skinned sheep, she is."

"Don't be impertinent! And disrespectful." Grandmama climbed out of bed and the cold air assailed her flesh through her nightgown. She grasped a robe and glared at the girl. "Don't speak of your betters like farmyard animals," she added for good measure. "I shall go and waken Miss Barrington myself. Where is Tilly?"

"Please, ma'am, she's got a terrible chill."

"Then leave her alone. You may fetch Miss Barrington's tea. And mine also. Fresh, mind. No leftovers."

"Yes, ma'am." The girl was happy to be

relieved of responsibility, and of having to tell the master and mistress herself. She did not like the old lady, nor did any of the other servants, miserable old body. Let her do the finding and the telling.

Grandmama marched along the corridor and banged with her closed hand on Maude's door. There was no answer, as she had expected. She would rather enjoy waking her up from a sound, warm sleep, for no good reason but a maid's hysterics.

She pushed the door open, went in, and closed it behind her. If there were going to be a bad tempered scene over the disturbance, better to have it privately.

The room was light, the curtains open.

"Miss Barrington!" she said very clearly.

There was no sound and no movement from the figure in the bed.

"Miss Barrington!" she repeated, considerably more loudly, and more peremptorily.

Still nothing. She walked over to the bed.

Maude lay on her back. Her eyes were closed, but her face was extremely pale, even a little blue, and she did not seem to be moving at all.

Grandmama felt a tinge of alarm. Drat the woman! She went a little closer and reached out to touch her, ready to leap back and apologize if her eyes flew open and she demanded to know what on earth Grand-mama thought she was doing. It was really inexcusable to place anyone in this embarrassing position. Gadding about in heathen places had addled her wits, and all sense of being an Englishwoman of any breeding at all.

The flesh that met her fingers was cold and quite stiff. There could be no doubt whatsoever that the stupid maid was correct. Maude was quite dead, and had been so probably most of the night.

Grandmama staggered backward and sat down very hard on the bedroom chair, suddenly finding it difficult to breathe. This was terrible. Quite unfair. First of all Maude had arrived, uninvited, and disrupted everything. Now she had died and made it even worse. They would have to spend Christmas in mourning! Instead of reds and golds, and carol singing, feasting, making merry, they would all be in black, mirrors covered, whispering in corners and being miserable and afraid. Servants were always afraid when there was a death in the house. Most likely Cook would give notice, and then where would they be? Eating cold meats!

She stood up. She had no reason to feel sad. It would be absurd. She had barely met Maude Barrington, certainly she had not known her. And there was nobody to feel sorry for. Her own family had not wanted her, even at Christmas, for heaven's sake! Perhaps they were tired of the endless stories about the bazaar at Marrakech and the Persian gardens or the boats on the Nile and the tombs of kings who had lived and died a thousand years or more before the first Christmas on earth, and worshipped gods of their own making, who had the heads of beasts.

But then her family could not have been nice people or they would not have turned Maude away at Christmas. They would have listened with affectation of interest, as Caroline and Joshua had done. Indeed, as she had done herself. She could imagine the water running over blue tiles in the sun. She did not know what jasmine smelled like, but no doubt it was beautiful. And to give her credit, Maude had loved the English countryside just as much, even in December. It was wretched that she should have died among people who were veritable strangers, taking her in out of charity because it was Christmas. Her own had not loved or wanted her.

Grandmama stood still in the middle of the bedroom with its flowered chintzes, heavy furniture, and dead ashes in the grate, and a hideous reality took her breath away. She herself was here out of charity as well, unloved and unwanted by anyone else. Caroline and Joshua were good people; that was why they had taken her in, not because they cared for her. They did not love her, they did not even like her. No one did. She knew that as well as she knew the feel of ice on her skin and the cold wind that cut to the bone.

She opened the door, her fingers fumbling on the handle, breath tight in her chest. Outside in the passage, she walked unsteadily to the other wing of the house, and Joshua and Caroline's room. She knocked more loudly than she had intended, and when Caroline opened the door to her she found her voice caught in her throat.

"The maid came and told me Maude died in the night." She gulped. Really this much emotion was ridiculous! She had barely known the woman. "I am afraid it is true."

Caroline looked stricken, but she could see from the old lady's face that there was no doubt. At her age she had seen enough death not to mistake it.

"You had better come into the dressing room and sit down," Caroline said gently. "I'll have Abby fetch you a cup of tea. I'm so sorry you had to be the one to find her."

She held out her arm to support Grandmama as she stumbled across the room and into the wide, warm dressing room with its seats and wardrobes and one of Caroline's gowns already layed out for the day. Grandmama was angry with herself for being so close to weeping. It must be the shock. It was most unpleasant to grow old. "Thank you," she said grudgingly.

Caroline helped her into one of the chairs and looked at her for a moment as if to make sure she were not going to faint. Then, as Grandmama glared back at her, she turned and went out to set in motion all the endless arrangements that would have to be made.

The old lady sat still. The maid brought her tea and poured it for her, encouraging her to drink it. It was refreshing, spreading warmth from the inside. But it changed nothing. Why was Maude dead? She had been in almost offensively good health the short time she had been here. What had she died of? Certainly not old age. Not any kind of wasting away or weakening. She could march like a soldier, and eat like one, too.

She closed her eyes and in her mind she saw Maude again, lying motionless in the bed. She did not look terrified or disturbed, or even in any pain. But there had been an empty bottle on the table beside her. Probably the peppermint water. The stupid woman had given herself indigestion guzzling all the nuts, just as Grandmama had told her she would. Why were some people so stupid? No self-control.

She drank the last of her tea and stood up. The room swayed around her for a moment. She took several deep breaths, then went out of the dressing room and back along the corridor to Maude's bedroom. There was no one else in sight. They must all be busy, and Caroline would be doing what she could to settle the staff. Staff always behaved erratically when someone died. At least one maid would have fainted, and someone would be having hysterics. As if there were not enough to do!

She opened the door and slipped inside quickly, closing it after her, then turned to look. Yes, she had been quite right, there was an empty bottle on the bedside table. She walked over and picked it up. It said "peppermint water" on the label, but just to be certain she took out the cork and sniffed it experimentally. It was quite definitely peppermint, clean and sharp, filling her nose.

Maude had brought it with her, with only one dose left. She must use it regularly.

Stupid woman! If she ate with any sense it would not be necessary. Curious that they should have it even in Arabia, or Persia, or wherever it was she had come from most recently. And the label was in English, too.

She looked at it again. It was printed with the name and address of a local apothecary in Rye, just a few miles away around the Dungeness headland.

But Maude had said she had not left Snave, in fact not had the chance to go out at all. So someone had given it to her, with one dose in it. Presumably that was to treat the result of eating the macadamia nuts! But one dose? How very odd. Especially when they could have been all but certain that she would require it. Surely no household would be short of so ordinary a commodity, especially over Christmas, when it could be guaranteed that people would overindulge? There was something about it that was peculiar.

She picked up the bottle again and, keeping it concealed in the folds of her skirt, returned to her room, where she hid it in the drawer with her underclothes.

Then, with Tilly's assistance, she dressed in the darkest clothes she had with her — not quite black, but a gray that in the winter light would pass for it. She went downstairs to face the day.

Caroline was in the withdrawing room before the fire. Joshua had gone to fetch the local doctor so that the necessary authorities could be satisfied.

"Are you all right, Mama-in-law?" she asked anxiously. "It is a terrible experience for you."

"It was a much worse experience for Maude!" Grandmama replied with tart candor. There were troubling thoughts in her mind, but she was not quite certain exactly what they were. She could not share them, especially with Caroline, who had never detected anything, as far as she knew. She might even wish to avoid scandal, and refuse even to consider it, and Maude deserved better than that! Perhaps it rested with Mariah Ellison, and no one else, to face the truth.

A few minutes later the doctor arrived and was taken upstairs.

"Heart failure," he informed them when he came down again. "Very sad. She seemed in excellent health otherwise."

"She was!" Grandmama said quickly, before anyone else could reply. "She was a world traveler, walked miles, rode horses, and even camels. She never spoke of any ailment at all."

"It can come without warning," the doctor said gently.

"An attack that kills?" Grandmama demanded. "She did not look as if she were in that kind of agony!"

"No," he agreed with a slight frown. "I think it more likely that her heart simply slowed and then stopped."

"Slowed and then stopped?" Grandmama said incredulously.

"Mama-in-law!" Caroline remonstrated.

"I think it may well have been peaceful," the doctor said to Grandmama. "If that is of comfort to you? Were you very fond of her?"

"She barely knew her!" Caroline said tartly.

"Yes, I was fond of her." Grandmama contradicted her, equally tartly.

"I'm very sorry." The doctor was still gentle. He turned to Joshua. "If I can assist with arrangements, of course I shall be happy to."

"Thank you," Joshua accepted.

"We shall have to inform the rest of her family," Grandmama said loudly. "Bedelia whatever-her-name-is."

"I have been thinking how on earth I can write such a letter," Caroline acknowledged. "What to say that will make it . . . *better* sounds absurd. If I simply say that we are terribly sad to inform them, will that be best?" She looked worried, and "sad" would be no exaggeration. There was a grief in her face that was quite genuine.

Grandmama's mind was racing. What was she allowing herself to think? Heart slowing down? Nuts that everyone knew were indigestible? One dose of peppermint water? Had Maude been murdered? Preposterous! That's what came of allowing one's daughter to marry a policeman. This was Caroline's fault. If she had been a mother of the slightest responsibility at all she would never have permitted Charlotte to do such a thing! Thomas Pitt, as a law enforcement official, was not a suitable husband. He had absolutely nothing to commend him, except possibly height?

But if someone like Pitt could solve a crime, then most certainly Grandmama could. She would not be outwitted by a gamekeeper's son, half her age!

And if Maude Barrington had been murdered, then Mariah Ellison would see that whoever had done so was brought to justice and answered to the last penny for such an act. Maude might have been an absurd woman, and a complete nuisance, but there was such a thing as justice.

Grandmama felt as if a light and a warmth had gone out of the air and a heaviness settled in its place, which she did not understand at all.

"You should not write," she said firmly to Caroline. "It is far too dreadful and sudden a thing to put in a letter, when apparently they live so near. Snake, isn't it? Or something like that."

"Snave," Caroline corrected. "Yes. It's about four or five miles away. Still well within the Marsh. Do you think I should go over and tell them myself?" Her face tightened. "Yes, of course you're right."

"No!" Grandmama said quickly. "I agree it should be done personally. After all, she was their sister, however they treated her. Perhaps they will even feel an overwhelming guilt now." She thought that extremely unlikely. They were obviously quite shameless. "But I will go. You have arrangements to make for Christmas, and Joshua would miss you. And I imagine I actually spent more time with Maude than you did anyway. I may be able to be of some comfort, inform them a little of her last days." She sounded sententious and she knew it. She watched Caroline's expression acutely. It would be a disaster if she were to come, too; in fact it would make the entire journey

51

a waste of time. In order to have a hope of accomplishing anything she would be obliged to tell Caroline what she suspected with increasing certainty the more she considered it.

A spark of hope lit in Caroline's eyes. "But that is a great deal to ask of you, Mama-in-law."

Of course she was dubious. Mariah Ellison had never in her life been known to discomfort herself on someone else's behalf. It was totally out of character. But then Caroline did not know her very well. For nearly twenty years they had lived under the same roof, and for all of it Grandmama had lived a lie. She had hidden her misery and self-loathing under the mantle of widowhood. But how could she have done anything else? The shame of her past continually burned inside her as if the physical pain were still raw and bleeding and she could barely walk. She had had to lie, for her son's sake. And the lie had grown bigger and bigger inside her, estranging her from everyone.

"You did not ask it of me," she said more sharply than she meant to. "I have offered. It is the answer that makes the greatest sense." Should she add that Caroline and Joshua had made her welcome here and it was a small repayment? No. Caroline would never believe that. They had allowed her in, she was not welcome, nor was she stupid enough to imagine that she could be. Caroline would be suspicious.

"I have nothing else to do," she added more realistically. "I am bored." That was believable. She was certainly not about to admit to Caroline, of all people, that she actually had admired Maude Barrington and felt a terrible anger that she should have been abandoned by her family, and very possibly murdered by one of them. She waited for Caroline's reaction. She must not push too hard.

"Are you certain you would not mind?" Caroline was still unconvinced.

"Quite certain," she replied. "It is still a pleasant morning. I shall compose myself, have a little luncheon, and then go. That is, if you can spare the carriage to take me there? I doubt there is any other way of travel in this benighted spot!" A sudden idea occurred to her. "Perhaps you fear that . . ."

"No," Caroline said quickly. "It is most generous of you, and I think entirely appropriate. It shows far more care than any letter could do, no matter how sincere, or well written. Of course the coachman will take you. As you say, the weather is still quite clement. This afternoon would be perfect. I do appreciate it."

Grandmama smiled, trying to show less triumph than she felt. "Then I shall prepare myself," she replied, finishing her tea and rising to her feet. She intended to remain at Snave for as long as it required to discover the truth of Maude's death, and to prove it. Knowing alone was hardly adequate. Her visit might well stretch into several days. She must succeed. It was not a matter of sentimentality, it was a matter of principle, and she was a woman to whom such things mattered.

■ ■ ■ ■

PART TWO

■ ■ ■ ■

The journey was bumpy and cold, even with a traveling rug wrapped around from the waist downward. There was a bitter, whining wind coming in off the sea, though now and again it cleared the sky of clouds. The light was chill and hard over the low-lying heath. This was the invasion coast where Julius Caesar had landed fifty-five years before the birth of Christ. No such thing as Christmas then! He had gone home and been murdered the following year. That had been by his own people too, those he had known and trusted for years.

Eleven centuries after that, William, Duke of Normandy, had landed with his knights and bowmen and killed King Harold at Hastings, just around the coast from here. Somehow she was faintly satisfied with Caesar coming. Rome had been the center of the world then. England had been proud to be part of that Empire. But William's invasion still rankled, which was silly, since it was the best part of a thousand years ago! But it was the last time England had been conquered, and it annoyed her.

King Philip of Spain's armada would probably have landed here too, if the wind had not destroyed it. And Napoleon Bonaparte. Only he went to Russia instead, which had proved to be a bad idea.

Was this a bad idea, too? Arrogant, stupid, the result of a fevered imagination? But how could she possibly turn back? She would look like a complete fool! To be disliked was bad enough. To be despised as well — or worse, pitied — would be unendurable.

Looking out of the carriage window as the sky darkened and the already lowering sun was smeared with gray, she could not imagine why anyone would choose to be here if they did not have to. Except Maude, of course! She thought these flat, wide spaces and wind-raging skies were beautiful with their banners of cloud, marsh grasses, and air that always smelled of salt.

Perhaps she did not remember it frozen solid, or so shrouded in fog that you could not make out your hand in front of your face! That was exactly what would be useful now, some dreadful weather, so she could not return to St. Mary in the Marsh for several days. She had undertaken a very big task, and the more she thought of it the bigger it seemed, and the more hopeless. It was in a way a comfort that she could not turn back, or she might have. She had no idea what these people were like, and not a shred of authority to back up what she was intending to do. Or to try. It might have been better after all if Charlotte were here. She had meddled so often surely she had acquired a knack for it by now?

But she wasn't here. Grandmama would have to make the best of it by herself. Forward regardless. She had intelligence and determination, which might be enough. Oh — and right on her side as well, of course. It was monstrous that Maude Barrington should have been murdered, if she had been? But whatever the truth of that, they had still turned her away, and at Christmas. That in itself was an unforgivable offense, and on Maude's behalf, she felt it to the core.

The distance was covered far too quickly. It was only a handful of miles, forty minutes' journey at a brisk trot, far less as the crow flew. Every lane seemed to double back on itself as if to circumnavigate each field and cross every ditch twice. The sky had cleared again and the light was long and low, making the shivering grass bright and casting networks of shadow through the bare trees when the carriage drove into the tiny village of Snave. There was really only one big house. The rest seemed to be cottages and farm buildings. Why in heaven's name would anyone choose to live here? It was no more than a widening in the road.

She took a deep breath to steady her nerves and waited with pounding heart for the coachman to open the door for her. A dozen times she had rehearsed what she was going to say, and now when she needed it, it had gone completely out of her mind.

Outside in the driveway the wind was like a knife-edge and she found herself rocking on her feet in the strength of it. She grasped onto her cloak to keep it from flying away, and stamped up to the front door, leaning heavily on her stick. The coachman pulled on the doorbell for her, and stood back to wait.

It was answered almost immediately. Someone must have seen the carriage arrive. An extremely ordinary-looking butler spoke to her civilly enough.

"Good afternoon," she replied. "I am Mrs. Mariah Ellison. Mr. Joshua Fielding, with whom Miss Barrington was staying, is my son-in-law." The exact nature of their relationship could be explained later, if necessary. "I am afraid I have extremely distressing news to bring to the family, the sort of thing that can really only be told in person."

He looked alarmed. "Oh, dear. Please do come in, Mrs. Ellison." He opened the door wider for her and backed away a little.

"Thank you," she accepted. "May I ask you the favor of a little warmth and refreshment for my coachman also, and perhaps water for the horses, and at least in the meantime, shelter from this rather cutting wind?"

"Of course! Of course! Do you . . ." He swallowed. "Do you have Miss Barrington with you?"

"No, indeed not," she replied, following him inside after a brief glance behind her to make certain that the coachman had heard, and would drive around to the stables and make himself known.

Inside the hall she could not help but glance around. It was not a house of London fashion; nevertheless it was well furnished and extremely comfortable. The floor was very old oak, stained dark with possibly centuries of use. The walls were paneled, but lighter, and hung with many paintings, mercifully not the usual portraits of generations of forebears with expressions sour enough to turn the milk. Instead they were glowing still lifes of fruit and flowers, and one or two pastoral scenes with enormous skies and restful cows. At least someone had had very good taste. It was also blessedly warm.

"The family is all together, ma'am," the butler continued gravely. "Would you perhaps prefer to tell Mrs. Harcourt this news in private? She is Miss Barrington's elder sister."

"Thank you. She will know best how to inform the rest of the family."

The butler thereupon led her to a doorway off to the side. He opened it to show her into a very agreeable room, lighting the lamps for her and poking up a fire, which had almost gone out. He placed a couple of pieces of coal on it judiciously, then excused himself and left. He did not offer her tea. Perhaps he was too alarmed at the news, even though he did not yet know what it was. Judging by his manner, he expected a disgrace rather than a tragedy — which in itself was interesting.

She stood by the fire, trying to warm herself. Her heart was still thumping and she had difficulty keeping her breath steady.

The door opened and a woman of great beauty came in, closing it behind her. She was perhaps sixty, with auburn hair softening to rather more gold than copper, and the clear, fair skin that so often goes with such coloring. Her features were refined, her eyes large and blue. Her mouth was perfectly shaped. She bore little resemblance to Maude. It was not easy to think of them as sisters. No one would have called Maude beautiful. What had made her face so attractive was intelligence, and a capacity for feeling and imagination, a soul of inner joy. There was no echo of such things in this woman's face. In fact she looked afraid, and angry. Her clothes were up to the moment in fashion, and perfectly cut with the obligatory shoulders and high crowned sleeves.

"Good afternoon, Mrs. Ellison," she said with cool politeness. "I am Bedelia Harcourt. My butler tells me that you have driven all the way from St. Mary in the Marsh with unfortunate news about my sister. I hope she has not" — she hesitated delicately — "embarrassed you?"

Grandmama felt a fury of emotion rise up inside her so violently she was overwhelmed by it, almost giddy. She wanted to rage at the woman, even slap her perfect face. However, that would be absurd and the last way to detect anything. She was quite sure Pitt would not have been so . . . so amateur!

"I'm so sorry, Mrs. Harcourt." She controlled herself with a greater effort than she had ever exercised over her temper before. "But the news I have is very bad indeed. That is why I came personally rather than have anyone write a letter to you." She watched intently to see if there were the slightest betraying foreknowledge in Bedelia's face, and saw nothing. "I am afraid Miss Barrington passed away in her sleep last night. I am so very sorry." That at least was sincere. She was amazed how sorry she was.

Bedelia stared at her as if the words had no meaning that she could grasp. "Passed away?" she repeated. She put her hand up to her mouth. "Maude? But she never even said she was ill! I should have known! Oh, how terrible. How very terrible."

"I am sorry," Grandmama said yet again. "The maid knocked on my door. I was in the same part of the house. I went to her immediately, but Miss Barrington must have died early in the night. She was . . . quite cold. We called a doctor, naturally."

"Oh, dear." Bedelia stepped backward and almost folded up into the chair behind her. It was a collapse, and yet it was oddly graceful. "Poor Maude. How I wish she had said something. She was too . . . too reticent . . . too brave."

Grandmama remembered Bedelia's letter to Joshua saying that she would not have Maude in the house because they had other important guests, and she found it extremely difficult not to remind her of that. But to do so would make an enemy of her, and then gaining any knowledge would be impossible. Really, this detecting required greater sacrifices than she had foreseen.

"I am deeply sorry for coming bearing such painful news," she said instead. "I cannot imagine what a shock it must be for you. I spent a little time with Miss Barrington and she was a delightful person. And I admit that to me she appeared to be in the most excellent health. I can understand your shock."

Bedelia raised her eyes and looked up at her. "She . . . she had lived abroad for some time, in very harsh climates. It must have affected her more than we appreciated. Possibly more than she appreciated herself."

Grandmama sat down in the other chair opposite Bedelia. "She spoke somewhat of Marrakech, and I believe Persia. And Egypt also. Was she there for some time?"

"Years," Bedelia replied, straightening up. "Since she left, shortly before I was married, and that is all but forty years ago. She must have lived in a style far more . . . injurious to her health than we had realized. Perhaps she did not fully know it herself."

"Perhaps not," Grandmama agreed. Then a thought occurred to her. Sitting here being pleasant and questioning nothing was unlikely to gain her any knowledge. Pitt would have done better. "Or maybe she was only too well aware that she was not in good health, and that is why she returned to England, and her family, the people to whom she was closest in the world?"

Bedelia's magnificent eyes opened wider and were momentarily as hard and cold as the midwinter sea.

Grandmama looked back at her without so much as blinking.

Bedelia let out her breath slowly. "I suppose you could be right. No such thought had crossed my mind. Like you, I imagined her to be in the most excellent health. It seems we were both tragically mistaken."

"She said nothing that could lead you to expect this?" Grandmama felt most discourteous to press the matter, but justice came before good manners.

Bedelia hesitated, as if she could not make up her mind how to answer. "I can think of nothing," she said after a moment. "I confess I am utterly devastated. My mind does not seem to function at all. I have never lost anyone so . . . so very close to me before."

"Your parents are still alive?" Grandmama said in amazement.

"Oh, no," Bedelia corrected herself quickly. "I meant of my own generation. My parents were excellent people, of course! But distant. A sister is . . . is very dear. Perhaps one only realizes it when they are gone. The void left behind is greater than one can conceive beforehand."

You are overplaying it, Grandmama thought to herself. You wouldn't even have her in the house! Outwardly she smiled. It was a totally artificial expression.

"You are very naturally suffering from shock," she commiserated. "When one's own generation passes away it is a reminder of mortality, the shadow of death across one's own path. I remember how I felt when my husband died." So she did — the most marvelous liberation of her life. Even if she could tell no one, and had to pretend to be devastated, and wear mourning for the rest of her days, like the Queen.

"Oh, I am sorry!" Bedelia said quickly. "You poor soul! And now you have come all the way in this weather to bring this news

67

to me personally. And I am sitting here without even offering you tea. My wits are completely scattered. I still have my beloved Arthur, how can I complain of anything? Perhaps poor Maude has gone to a better place. She was never a happy creature. I shall allow that to be my comfort." She rose to her feet a trifle unsteadily.

"Thank you, that is most kind of you," Grandmama accepted. "I must admit it has been a dreadful day, and I am quite exhausted. I am so glad you have your husband. He will no doubt be a great strength to you. One can be very . . . alone."

Bedelia's face softened in concern. "I can scarcely imagine it. I have always been so fortunate. This room is a little chill. Would you care to come through to the withdrawing room where it is far warmer? We shall all take tea and consider what must be done. Of course if you prefer to return to St. Mary in the Marsh as soon as possible, we shall understand."

"Thank you," Grandmama said weakly. "I should be most grateful for as long a rest as I may take, without imposing upon you. And certainly tea would be very welcome." She also rose to her feet, as unsteadily as she could without risking actually falling over, which would be ridiculous, and only to be resorted to if all else failed.

Bedelia led the way back across the hall to the withdrawing room, and Grandmama followed, refusing to offer her arm to the younger woman. She must be consistent about her own exhaustion or she might be disbelieved.

The withdrawing room was spacious also and the warmth from the enormous fire engulfed them both as soon as they entered. There was too much furniture for more modern tastes; carved sideboards, heavily stuffed sofas and chairs with antimacassars on all of them. There were also hard-backed chairs by the walls with fat leather-upholstered seats and slightly bowed legs, and several footstools with tassels around the edges. A brightly colored Turkish rug was worn duller where possibly generations of feet had passed. On the walls were embroidered samplers, paintings of every variety large and small, and several stuffed animals in glass cases, even a case full of butterflies as dry as silk. The colors were mostly hot: golds, browns, and ocher reds. Caroline would have thought it oppressive. Grandmama was annoyed to find it very agreeable, indeed almost familiar.

The people in it were entirely another matter. She was introduced to them, and

Bedelia was obliged to explain her presence to them.

"My dears." Everyone turned to her. "This is Mrs. Ellison, who has most graciously come in person rather than send a message to tell us some terrible news." She turned to Grandmama. "I am certain you would prefer to sit down, perhaps by the fire? May I introduce you to my sister, Mrs. Agnes Sullivan." She indicated a woman whose superficial resemblance to her was explained by the relationship. They appeared of a similar height, although Mrs. Sullivan did not rise as the three men had done. Her coloring had probably been similar to Bedelia's in youth, but now it was scattered with more gray and the dark areas were duller. Her features were less finely chiseled, and her expression, apart from a certain sadness, was much gentler. Her clothes, although well cut, managed to look commonplace.

"How do you do, Mrs. Sullivan," Grandmama said formally.

"And her husband, Mr. Zachary Sullivan," Bedelia continued.

Zachary bowed very slightly. He was a slender man with brown hair, now graying at the temples. His face also was pleasant, but marked by a certain sense of loss, as if he had failed to achieve something that mattered to him too much to forget.

"My daughter-in-law, Clara, and my son, Randolph," Bedelia continued, indicating in one sweep a young man whose coloring resembled hers, although his features did not, being considerably stronger and blunter. The woman beside him was handsome enough in a powerful way, dark-haired, dark-eyed, and with brows rather too heavy.

Bedelia smiled, in spite of the occasion. "And my husband Arthur," she finished, turning to a remarkably handsome man whose dark hair was now iron gray. His eyes held a wit and life that captured attention instantly, and his smile at Grandmama showed perfect teeth.

"Welcome to Snave, Mrs. Ellison," he said warmly. "I am sorry it is distressing news that brings you. May I offer you tea, or would you prefer something more robust, such as a glass of sherry? I know it is early, but the wind is miserable and you have to be chilled, and perhaps tired also."

"That is most generous of you, and understanding." Grandmama made her way over to the fire, and the seat Zachary had left vacant for her. Whoever was guilty of having killed Maude, if indeed someone had, she hoped it was not Arthur Harcourt.

"What is it you have to tell us, Mrs. Ellison?" Agnes Sullivan asked with a tremor in her voice.

"I am afraid Miss Barrington passed away in her sleep last night," Grandmama replied solemnly. "I believe it must have been peaceful, and she seemed to be in excellent health and spirits right until the last moment. She made no remark as to feeling unwell. I am so sorry." She glanced rapidly from one to the other of them, trying to judge their reactions. Not that she was sure she could tell guilt from shock anyway, or from grief for that matter.

Zachary looked least surprised, rather more puzzled, as if he had not fully understood the meaning of her words.

Agnes gave a gasp and her hand flew to her mouth in a gesture of stopping herself from crying out, oddly like Bedelia's five minutes before. She was very pale.

"Poor Aunt Maude," Randolph murmured. "I'm so sorry, Mama." He looked at Bedelia with concern.

Clara Harcourt said nothing. Perhaps as one who had barely known Maude she felt it more appropriate not to speak.

Arthur Harcourt's olive complexion was a muddy color, neither white nor gray, and his eyes seemed to have lost focus. What was he feeling? Was that the horror of guilt now that the act was real and not merely dreamed?

"I am sorry to bring you such news." Grandmama felt compelled to fill in the silence that seemed to choke the room. The mere flickering of the fire sounded like a sheet torn in the wind.

"It . . . it was good of you," Agnes stammered. "Such a terrible thing for you . . . a guest in your house . . . a virtual stranger."

Suddenly a quite brilliant idea lit in Grandmama's mind. It went up like a flare of light. She could almost feel the heat of it in her face. "Oh, not at all!" she said with feeling. "We talked for hours, Maude and I." She was stunned at her own audacity. "She told me so much about . . . oh, of any number of things. Her feelings, her experiences, where she had been and the people she had met." She waved her hands for emphasis. "Believe me, there are those I have been acquainted with for years about whom I know far less. I have never made such excellent friends with anyone so rapidly, or with such a natural affection." That was a monstrous lie — wasn't it? "I must admit her trust in me was most heartwarming, and that was a great deal the reason why I could not possibly allow anyone else to come to you now," she hurried on. "I shall never forget Maude, or the confidence she placed in me regarding her life and its meaning." It was an extraordinary feeling to have made such statements as if they were true, as if she and Maude had become instant and total friends.

She realized with a flutter of absurdity, even of sweetness, that it was not completely a lie. Maude had told her more of meaning in a couple of days than most of her acquaintances had in years, although not the personal details she implied to her wretched family!

And grudgingly, like the lancing of a boil, she admitted that she had actually liked Maude, at least more than she had expected to, considering the gross imposition of having her in Caroline's home for Christmas — uninvited!

Bedelia stared at her incredulously. "Really? But you knew her for barely a day . . . or two!"

"But we had little to do but talk to each other. She was fascinating at the luncheon and dinner table, but even more so when we were out walking, just the two of us. I was very flattered that she should tell me so much. I found myself speaking equally frankly to her, and finding her most gentle and free from critical judgment. It was a quite . . . quite wonderful experience," she added too quickly. She said it purely to frighten them into believing she knew something of whoever it was who had murdered Maude, if indeed they had. This was a deviousness added to her new grief. She intended them to think her too desolate to consider the long carriage ride in the dark to go home again!

She also found, to her dismay, that she wished quite painfully that it were all true. She had not been anything like such friends with Maude. Nor had she confided in her the agonies of her own life, the shame she had carried for years that she had not had the courage to leave her abusive husband and flee abroad as his first wife had done!

But it was startlingly sweet to think that Maude might have sympathized rather than despising her for a coward, as she despised herself. There would have been nothing in the world more precious than a friend who understood. But that was idiotic! Maude would never have submitted herself to such treatment.

"Then you grieve with us," Arthur said gently, intruding across her thoughts. "Please feel welcome here, and do not consider the journey back to St. Mary tonight. It will be dark quite soon, and you must be both tired and distressed. I am certain we can supply anything you might need, such as a nightgown and toiletries. And of course we have plenty of room."

"Since Lord Woollard has left, the guest room is perfectly available," Clara put in quickly.

"Oh yes, the guest who was staying with you before, when poor Maude arrived," Grandmama noted. "How very kind of you. I really should be most grateful. May I inform my coachman of your generosity, so he can return to St. Mary? It is possible Mr. and Mrs. Fielding may require the coach tomorrow. And of course if they do not hear, they may worry that something has happened to me."

"Naturally," Arthur agreed. "Would you care to tell him yourself, or shall I have the butler inform him?"

"That would be very kind of you," she accepted. "And ask him to tell Mrs. Fielding of your graciousness, and that I am perfectly well . . . just . . . just so grieved."

"Of course." Now the die was cast. What on earth was she thinking of? Her stomach lurched and her mouth was dry.

She sipped the excellent sherry she had

been given and allowed herself to bask for a moment in its delicious warmth. She had embarked upon an adventure. That is the way she must look at it. She was still angry that Maude had been treated so appallingly, whether it included murder or not, although she really thought it might! And she was tired and grieved, quite truly grieved. Maude had been too full of life to die, too joyous in tasting every good experience to give it up so soon. And no one should be unwanted by their own, whatever the reason.

What was the reason? Who in this comfortable room with its roaring fire, its silver tea tray and overstuffed sofas, had wanted Maude out of the house? And why had the rest of them allowed it? Were they all guilty of something? Secrets so terrible they would kill to hide them? They looked so perfectly innocuous, even ordinary. Good heavens, what wickedness can lie beneath a smiling exterior as commonplace as a slice of bread!

Later a maid showed her to the spare bedroom. It was warm and agreeably furnished with a four-poster bed, heavy curtains of wine brocade, another red Turkish carpet, and plenty of carved oak furniture. A very fine ewer with painted flowers on it held fresh water. There was a matching bowl for washing in and on the stand beside them plenty of thick towels with which to dry oneself. There was no way of telling whether Lord Woollard, or anyone else, had occupied it recently. But she would take the opportunity to see how many guest rooms there were so she would know whether Maude could have been accommodated had they wished to. She tiptoed along the corridor, feeling like a sneak thief, and cautiously tried the handles and opened the doors of the two other rooms. They were both bedrooms, and both presently unoccupied. So much for that lie.

She returned to her own room, her hands trembling a little and her knees weak. She sat down. Then another idea struck her. She opened the small cupboard beside the bed, and found lavender water, a vial with a couple of doses of laudanum, and a full bottle of peppermint water! The cork was jammed in tightly, but more telling than that, there was a film of dust over it. It had not been purchased in the last couple of days since Maude had left! So much for being out of it! That put a new complexion on Maude's single dose! Had there been something else in it, disguised by the pungent taste? And the macadamia nuts to make her require it? She closed the cupboard door and sat down heavily on the bed. So far everything had gone quite marvelously. But there was a great deal to do. She must ascertain if Maude had indeed been murdered, if so by whom, precisely how — and it would hardly be complete if she did not also know why! How could she possibly do all that before they politely sent her home? Pitt had no challenge of mere hours in which to solve his cases! He went on for days! Sometimes even weeks! And he had the authority to ask questions and demand answers — not necessarily true ones, of course. She was going to have to be much cleverer than he was! It might not be quite so easy as she had assumed.

Still, so far, so good. And she was much too angry to give up.

However, later on, when in ordinary circumstances she would have been changing for dinner, she was overwhelmed by the strangeness of her surroundings and all the events that had occurred in the last few days. This time last week she had been in London with Emily and Jack, as usual. Then she had been upheaved and sent to St. Mary in the Marsh. She had barely settled to accepting that when Maude Barrington had arrived. That was almost accommodated, and Maude died, without the slightest warning of any sort!

Grandmama had been the only one to perceive that it might well not be natural, but a crime, the most appalling of all crimes, and there was no one else but herself to find justice for it. And here she was sitting quite alone in a house full of strangers, at least one of whom she was now convinced was a murderer. Added to that she had not even fresh underclothes or a nightgown to sleep in. They had offered to lend her something, but all the women in the family were at least three or four inches taller than she was, and thinner as well, by more inches than that! She must have taken leave of her wits. Certainly she could never admit any of this to Caroline! Or anybody else. They'd have her locked up.

There was a knock on the door and she started so violently she gulped and gave herself hiccups.

"Come in!" she said, hiccuping again.

It was the housekeeper, to judge from her black dress, lace cap, and the cluster of keys hanging from her waist. She was short and rather stout, exactly Grandmama's own build.

"Good evening, ma'am," she said very agreeably. "I'm Mrs. Ward, the housekeeper.

It was very good of you to come personally with the sad news. It must have inconvenienced you very much."

"Her death grieved me," Grandmama answered frankly, relieved that it was a servant, not one of the family. "To come and tell you personally seemed no more than the obvious thing to do. She died among strangers, even if they were people who liked her immediately, and very much."

Mrs. Ward's face colored as if with considerable emotion she felt obliged to hide. "I'm very glad you did," she said with a tremble in her voice. She blinked rapidly.

"You knew her," Grandmama deduced. She made herself smile. "You must be grieving as well."

"Yes, ma'am. I was a maid here when I was a girl. Miss Maude would have been sixteen then."

"And Mrs. Harcourt?" Grandmama asked shamelessly. She must detect! Time would not wait upon niceties.

"Oh, eighteen she was. And such a beauty as you've never seen."

Grandmama looked at the housekeeper's face. There was no light in it. She might respect Bedelia Harcourt, even be loyal to her, but she did not like her as she had Maude. That was something to remember.

Servants said little, good ones seldom said anything at all, but they saw just about everything.

"And Mrs. Sullivan?"

"Oh, she was only thirteen, just a schoolgirl, all ink and books and clumsiness, but full of enthusiasm, poor girl. The governess was always trying to get her to walk with the dictionary on her head, but she kept losing it."

"Dictionary?"

"Only for the weight of it! Miss Agnes was perfectly accurate with her spelling. But that's all in the past. Long ago." She blinked rapidly again. "I just came to say that if there is anything I can get for you, I should be happy to." She had an air of sincerity as if her words were far more than mere politeness, or even obedience to Bedelia's request.

"Thank you," Grandmama replied. "I . . . I'm afraid I have none of the usual necessities with me." Dare she ask for a clean petticoat or chemise?

Mrs. Ward looked embarrassed. "There is no difficulty in the least finding you toiletries, Mrs. Ellison. I was thinking of . . . of more personal things. If you'll forgive my saying so, it seems to me that you and I are much the same height. If you would not be offended, ma'am, you might borrow one or two of my . . . my clothes. It would give us the chance to . . . care for yours and return them to you?" She was very pink; as if afraid already that she had presumed.

Grandmama was suddenly touched by the woman's kindness. It seemed perfectly genuine, and perhaps added to because she had cared for Maude. "That is extremely generous of you to offer," she said warmly. "I would be most grateful. I have nothing but what I stand up in. It was the last thing on my mind as I left this morning."

Mrs. Ward colored even more, but most obviously with relief. "Then I shall see that they are brought. Thank you, ma'am."

"It is I who thank you," Grandmama said, startled by her own courtesy, and rather liking it. It flashed into her mind that in a way Maude's death had given her the opportunity to begin a new life herself, even if only for a day or two. No one here in Snave knew her. She could be anything she wanted to be. It was a dizzying sort of freedom, as if the past did not exist. She suddenly smiled at the housekeeper again. "You have extraordinary courtesy," she added.

Mrs. Ward blushed again, then she retreated. Fifteen minutes later she returned carrying two black dresses, an assortment of undergarments, and a nightgown.

With the assistance of one of the maids assigned to help her, a most agreeable girl, Grandmama was able to dress for dinner in very respectable black bombazine, well cut and modest in fashion, as suited an elderly lady or a housekeeper. She put on her own jet and pearl jewelry, serving the double purpose of lifting the otherwise somberness of the attire, and also being classic mourning jewelry. She had a lot of such things, from the period when she had made a great show of being a widow.

Added to which they were really very pretty. The seed pearls made them dainty.

She went down the stairs and across the hall to the withdrawing room. She could hear lively conversation from inside, amazingly so, but she did not know the voices well enough to tell who they belonged to.

She opened the door, and they all ceased instantly, faces turned toward her. The gentlemen rose to their feet and welcomed her. The ladies looked at her, made polite noises, observed the change of gown but did not remark on it.

Conversation resumed, but stiffly, with a solemnity completely different from that before she had come in.

"I hope you are comfortable, Mrs. Ellison?" Bedelia inquired.

"Very, thank you," Grandmama replied, sitting in one of the overstuffed chairs. "You are most generous." Again she smiled.

"It is fortunate Lord Woollard left when he did," Clara observed.

Grandmama wondered whether that remark was made to convince her that they had not had sufficient accommodation for more than one further guest at a time, hence the need to turn Maude away. If so, it was ridiculous. She knew there were at least two more rooms unoccupied. And family should be first, most particularly when they were returning from a long time away.

"Indeed," she said, as if she were agreeing. "Is he a close friend? He will be very sad to hear of Maude's demise."

"He never met her," Bedelia said hastily. "I do not think we need to cloud his Christmas by telling him bad news that can scarcely be of concern to him."

So they had entertained a mere acquaintance in Maude's place!

"I thought perhaps he was a relative," Grandmama murmured.

Arthur smiled at her. "Not at all. A business acquaintance." He sounded tired, a strain in his voice, a kind of bitter humor. "Sent actually to assess whether I should be offered a peerage or not. See if I am suitable."

"Of course you are suitable!" Bedelia said sharply. "It is a formality. And I daresay he was pleased to get out of the city and visit us for a day or two. Cities are so . . . grubby when it snows."

"It isn't snowing," he pointed out.

She ignored him. "At least his visit was not marred by tragedy."

"Or anything else," Clara added quietly.

"I think it will snow," Agnes offered, glancing toward the curtained windows. "The wind has changed and the clouds were very heavy before sunset."

Grandmama was delighted. Snow might mean she could not leave tomorrow, if it were sufficiently deep. "Oh dear," she said with pretended anxiety. "I did not notice. I do hope I am not imposing on you?"

"Not in the slightest," Bedelia assured her. "You say you were a friend of Maude's, even on so short an acquaintance. How could you not be welcome?"

"Of course," Agnes agreed again, echoing Bedelia. "You said Maude spoke to you a great deal? We saw her so little, perhaps it would not be too distressing if we were to ask you what she told you of her . . . travels?" She looked hastily at Bedelia.

"That is . . . if it is seemly to discuss! I do not wish to embarrass you in any way at all."

What on earth was Agnes imagining? Orgies around the campfire?

"Perhaps . . . another time," Arthur said shakily, his voice hoarse. "If indeed it does snow, you may be here with us long enough to . . ." He trailed off.

"Quite," Bedelia agreed, without looking at him.

Zachary apologized. "We are all overwrought," he explained. "This is so unexpected. We hardly know how to . . . believe it."

"We had no idea at all that she was ill," Randolph spoke for the first time since Grandmama had come into the room. "She seemed so . . . so very alive . . . indestructible."

"You no more than met her, my dear," Bedelia said coolly.

Grandmama turned to her in surprise.

"Maude left before my son was born," Bedelia explained, as if an intrusive question had been asked. "I think you do not really understand what an . . . an extraordinary woman she was." Her use of the word *extraordinary* covered a multitude of possibilities, most of them unpleasant.

Grandmama did not reply. She must detect! The room was stiff with emotion. Grief, envy, anger, above all fear. Did she detect the odor of scandal? For heaven's sake, she was not achieving much! She had no proof that it had been murder, only a certainty in her own suspicious mind.

"No," she said softly. "Of course I didn't know how extraordinary she was. I spoke with her and listened to her memories and feelings, so very intense, a woman of remarkable observation and understanding. But as you say, it was only a short time. I have no right to speak as if I knew her as you must have, who grew up with her." She let the irony of the forty-year gap hang in the air. "I imagine when she was abroad she wrote wonderful letters?"

There was an uncomfortable silence, eloquent in itself. So Maude had not written to them in the passionate and lyrical way she had spoken at St. Mary. Or she had, and for some reason they chose to ignore it.

She plowed on, determined to stir up something that might be of meaning. "She had traveled as very few people, men or women, can have done. A collection of her letters would be of interest to many who do not have such opportunities. Or such remarkable courage. It would be a fitting monument to her, do you not think?"

Agnes drew in her breath with a gasp, and looked at Bedelia. She seemed helpless to answer without her approval. A lifetime habit forged in childhood? Perhaps forged was the right word, it seemed to fetter her like iron. It made Grandmama furious, with Agnes and with herself. It was a coward's way, and she knew cowardice intimately, as one knows one's own face in the glass.

Clara turned to her husband, then her mother-in-law, expecting some response.

But it was Arthur who answered.

"Yes, it would," he agreed.

"Arthur!" Bedelia said crisply. "I am sure Mrs. Ellison means well, but she really has no idea of the extent or the nature of Maude's . . . travels, or the unsuitability of making them public."

"Have you?" Arthur asked, his dark brows raised.

"I beg your pardon?" Bedelia said coolly.

"Have you any idea of Maude's travels?" he repeated. "I asked you if she wrote, and you said that she didn't." He did not accuse her of lying, but the inevitability of the conclusion was heavy in the air. She sat pale-faced, tight-lipped.

It was Clara who broke the silence. "Do you think it will still be acceptable for us to have the Matlocks and the Willowbrooks to dine with us on Christmas Eve, Mama-in-law? Or to go to the Watch Night services at Snargate? Or would people think us callous?"

"I don't suppose we can," Agnes said sadly. "I was looking forward to it too, my dear." She looked at Clara, not at Zachary who had drawn in his breath to say something.

"Death does not alter Christmas," Bedelia responded after a moment's thought. "In fact Christmas is the very time when it means least. It is the season in which we celebrate the knowledge of eternity, and the mercy of God. Of course we shall go to the Watch Night services in Snargate, and show a bond of courage and faith, and solidarity as a family. Don't you think so, my dear?" She looked at Arthur again, as if the previous conversation had never taken place.

"It would seem very appropriate," he answered to the room in general, no discernible emotion in his voice.

"Oh I'm so glad," Agnes responded, smiling. "And we have so much to be grateful for, it seems only right."

Grandmama thought it an odd remark. For what were they so grateful, just now? The fact that Lord Woollard had considered

Arthur suitable for a peerage? Could that matter in the slightest, compared with the death of a sister? Of course it could! Maude had not been home for forty years, and they had considered her absent permanently. She had chosen to return at a highly inconvenient time, otherwise they would not have dispatched her to stay with Joshua and Caroline. Was there really some family scandal she might speak of, and ruin such a high ambition?

Any further speculation on that subject was interrupted by the announcement of dinner. The meal was excellent, and richer than anything Caroline had offered.

Conversation at the table centered on other arrangements for Christmas, and how they might be affected either by Maude's death, or the weather. They skirted around the issue of a funeral, and when or where it should be conducted, but it hung in the air unsaid, like a coldness, as if someone had left a door open.

Grandmama stopped listening to the words and concentrated instead upon the intonation of voices, the ease or tension in hands, and above all the expression in a face when the person imagined they were unnoticed.

Clara appeared relieved, as if an anxiety

had passed. Perhaps the visit of Lord Woollard had made her nervous. She might be less confident than she appeared. Had she been socially clumsy or otherwise unacceptable? Since her husband was the only heir, that would have been a serious problem. Perhaps she came from a more ordinary background than the rest of the family and had previously made errors, or her mother was one of those women ruthlessly ambitious for their daughters, and no achievement was great enough?

Zachary did not say a great deal, and she saw him look at Bedelia more often than she would have expected. There was an admiration in him, a sense of awe. For her beauty? She was certainly far better looking than poor Agnes. She had a glamour, an air of femininity, mystery, almost power, that confidence gave her. Grandmama watched her as well, and in spite of herself.

What was it like to be beautiful? There were not many women so blessed, certainly she had never been so herself, and neither were Agnes nor Maude. Clara was no more than handsome. Luminous, heart-stopping beauty was very rare. Even Bedelia did not have that.

Grandmama had seen it once or twice, and one did not forget it. Emily's great-aunt by her first marriage, Lady Vespasia Cumming-Gould, had possessed it. Even in advanced years it was still there, unmistakable as a familiar song — one note, and the heart brings it all back.

Why did Zachary still watch Bedelia? Ordinary masculine fascination with beauty? Or good manners, because this was her house?

Arthur did not watch her the same way.

Agnes looked at both of them, and seemed to see it also. There was a sadness in her eyes. Was it an awareness that she could never compete? Perhaps that was the sense of failure Grandmama detected, and understood. She knew it well: a plain face, no magic in the eyes or the voice, above all the knowledge of not being loved.

Envy? Even hate, over the years? Why? Simply beauty? Could it matter so much? Very few women were more than pleasing in their youth, and perhaps gaining a little sense of style, or even better, wit, in their maturity. And she had not been left on the shelf. But sisters did compete. It was inevitable. Was money also involved, and now a peerage, too?

The conversation continued around her, concern for those who would be alone over the Christmas period and possibly in need, those whose health was poor, anyone to whom they could or should give a small gift. Would the weather deteriorate?

"Do you often get shut in by the snow?" Grandmama inquired with interest. "It must be a rather frightening experience."

"Not at all," Zachary assured her. "We will be quite safe. We have food and fuel, and it will not be for more than a day or two. But please don't concern yourself. If it happens at all, it will be in January and February. You know the old saying 'As the days get longer, the weather gets stronger.' " He smiled, transforming his face from its earlier gravity to a surprising warmth.

She smiled back, enjoying the sudden and inexplicable sense of freedom it gave her. "I have found it very often true," she agreed. "And I am sure you are quite wise enough to guard against any possible need. It was rather more such things as someone falling ill that I was thinking of. But I daresay that is a difficulty for all people who live in the wilder and more beautiful country areas."

She continued being charming. It was like having a new toy. She turned to Bedelia. "You know, Mrs. Harcourt, I would never have seen Romney Marsh as anything more than a very flat coast, rather vulnerable, with a permanent smell of the sea, until I met

Miss Barrington. But on our walks I saw how she was aware of so much more! She spoke of the wildflowers in the spring, and the birds. She knew the names of a great many of them, you know, and their habits. The water birds especially." She was inventing at least part of this as she was going along. It was exhilarating. The surprised and anxious faces around her increased her sense of adventure.

She drew in her breath and went on. "I had never realized before how perfectly everything fits into its own place in the scheme of things."

"Really?" Bedelia said, her voice almost expressionless. "It is an interest she had developed recently. In fact, since she left England altogether. She must have gained it from reading. Except perhaps in her early childhood, she never saw them in life."

"She did not go walking a great deal?" Grandmama asked innocently.

"She was only here for a matter of hours," Bedelia informed her. "She did not have time to go out at all. Surely she told you that she arrived without giving us any prior warning, and we were thus unable to accommodate her. Do you imagine we would have asked Joshua Fielding to offer his hospitality were it possible for us to do so ourselves?"

So she was correct! Maude had been given the single dose of peppermint water by someone in the house. She must think very rapidly. Better to retreat than to cause an argument, much as the words stuck in her mouth. Was it better to be considered a fool and of no danger at all, or as a highly knowledgeable woman who needed to be watched? She must decide immediately. She could not be both, and time was short.

Bedelia was waiting. They were all looking at her. A brilliant idea flashed into her mind. She could be both apparently stupid, and extremely clever — if she affected to be a little deaf!

She drew in a breath to say so, and apologize for it. Then just before she did, she had another thought of infinitely greater clarity. If she were to claim to be deaf then any evidence she gained could later be denied!

She smothered her pride, a thing she had never done before, except on that unmentionable occasion when her own past had loomed up like a corpse out of the river. But if she had survived that, then nothing this family could do to her would ever make a dent in her inner steel.

"You are quite right," she said meekly. "I had forgotten she had been away so very

96

long. If she had no interest before, then it must have been acquired entirely by reading. Perhaps she was homesick for the wide skies, the salt wind, and the sound of the sea?"

There was a flash of victory in Bedelia's eyes, a knowledge of her own power. Grandmama felt it as keenly as if it had been a charge of electricity between them such as one is pricked by at times if one touches certain metals when the air is very dry. She had read that predatory animals scented blood in the same way, and it gave her a shiver of fear and intense knowledge of vulnerability, which made life suddenly both sweet and fragile.

Was that what Agnes had known all her life? Or was she being fanciful? What about Maude? Was she crushed, too? Was that really why she had left England, and everything familiar that she unquestionably loved, and gone to all kinds of ancient, barbaric, and splendid other lands, where she neither knew anyone nor was known? A desperate escape?

Perhaps there was very much more here, beneath the surface, than she had dreamed, even when she had stood in the bedroom beside Maude's dead body this morning?

Bedelia was smiling. "Perhaps she was,"

she agreed aloud. "But she could have chosen to live by the sea if she had wished to. Poor Maude had very little sense of how to make decisions, even the right ones. It is most unfortunate."

"We were hoping to go out far more, later, when she returned . . ." Agnes glanced at Bedelia. "In the New Year . . . or . . . or whenever we were certain . . . ," she trailed off, knowing that somehow she had put her foot in it.

Grandmama stared at her, willing her to explain.

Bedelia sighed impatiently. "Agnes, dear, you really do let your tongue run away with you!" She turned to Grandmama in exasperation. "You had better know the truth, Mrs. Ellison, or you will feel that we are a cruel family. And it is not so at all. Maude is our middle sister, and she was always unruly, the one who had to draw attention to herself by being different. It happens in families at times. The eldest have attention because they are first, the youngest because they are the babies, the middle ones feel left out, and they show off, to use a common term."

"Maude was not a show-off," Arthur corrected her. "She was an enthusiast. Whatever she did, it was with a whole heart. There was nothing affected or contrived in her."

Bedelia did not look away from Grandmama. "My husband is a man of extraordinarily generous spirit. It is his work for the less fortunate for which Her Majesty is offering him a peerage. I am immensely proud of him, because it is for the noblest of reasons, nothing tawdry like finance, or political support." She smiled patiently. "But occasionally his judgment is rather more kind than accurate. It was apparent as soon as she arrived that Maude had traveled in places where manners and customs are quite different from ours. I'm afraid that even her language was not such that we could subject our other guests to her . . . her more colorful behavior. We knew that Joshua, being on the stage, might be more tolerant of eccentricity. Of course we could not know that you also would be staying with him, and if Maude has shocked you or made you uncomfortable, then we are guilty of having caused that, and on behalf of all of us, I apologize. Our inconsideration in that regard is what has been disturbing Agnes."

Agnes smiled, but there were tears in her eyes.

"I see." Grandmama tried to imagine Maude as an embarrassment so severe as to be intolerable. She did not know Lord Wool-lard. Perhaps he was insufferably pompous. There certainly were people so consumed by their own emotional inadequacy and imagined virtue as to take offense at the slightest thing. And the Maude she had met would find a certain delight in puncturing the absurd, the self-important, and above all the false. It would be a scene to be avoided. If Arthur Harcourt had done as much for others as Bedelia said, then he was deserving of recognition, and more importantly the added power to do more good that such an accolade would offer him.

"I'm sure you do," Bedelia said gently.

"All families seem to have their difficult members," Zachary added ruefully.

Grandmama had an unpleasant feeling that in her family it was she herself. Although Caroline was now giving her some competition, marrying an actor so much younger than herself! And there was Charlotte, of course, and her policeman!

A short while later the ladies retired to the withdrawing room and she learned little more of interest. She considered inquiring after people's health, but could think of no way of approaching the subject without being catastrophically obvious. She was extremely tired. It had been one of the longest days of her life, beginning with tragedy and horror, and ending with mystery, and the growing certainty in her mind that someone in this house had altered Maude's medicine. Exactly how it had been achieved, and with what, she had yet to ascertain. Even more important to her was why? Maude had been successfully sent to stay with Joshua. Lord Woollard had been and gone. What was the element so precious, or so terrible, that it was worth murder?

She excused herself, thanked them again for their hospitality, and went up to her room. Please heaven it would snow tonight, or in some other way make it impossible for her to leave. There was so much she had to learn. This detection matter was more difficult than she had supposed, and against her will she was being drawn into other people's lives. She cared about Maude, there was no use denying that anymore. She disliked Bedelia and had felt the strength of her power. She was sorry for Agnes without knowing why. Arthur intrigued her. In spite of all that was said about him, his success and his goodness to others, she felt an unnamed emotion that disturbed her. It did not fit in.

Randolph and Clara were still too undefined, except that Clara had great social ambitions! Could that possibly be enough to inspire murder?

It was all swirling around in her head as she put on the housekeeper's nightgown and climbed into the bed, intending to weigh it all more carefully, and instead fell asleep almost immediately.

The following morning she slept in, and was embarrassed to waken with the chambermaid standing at the foot of the bed with tea on a tray, and an inquiry as to what she would care for, for breakfast.

Would two lightly boiled eggs and some toast be possible?

Indeed it would, with the greatest pleasure.

After enjoying it, in spite of the circumstances and the thoughts that occupied her mind, she rose and washed. She dressed in the housekeeper's other black gown, again with the chambermaid's assistance, and found she rather enjoyed talking to her. Then she made her way downstairs.

She met Agnes in the hall. She was wearing outdoor clothes and apparently about to leave.

"Good morning, Mrs. Ellison," she said hastily. "I do hope you slept well? Such a distressing time for you. I hope you were comfortable? And warm enough?"

"I have never been more comfortable," Grandmama replied with honesty. "You are most generous. I do not believe I stirred all night. Are you about to go out?"

"Yes. I have a few jars of jams and chutneys to take to various friends. Nearby villages, you know? I am afraid the weather does not look promising."

Grandmama had another burst of illumination, of double worth. She could catch Agnes alone, unguarded by Bedelia, and if the weather did not oblige by snowing them in, she could affect to have caught a slight chill to prevent her returning to St. Mary in the Marsh tomorrow, or worse, this afternoon.

"May I come with you?" she asked eagerly. "I am not here beyond this brief Christmas period, and I would so love to see a little of the outside. It is quite unlike London. So much wider . . . and cleaner. The city always seems grubby when the snow has been trodden, and everything is stained with smoke from so many chimney fires."

"But of course!" Agnes said with pleasure. "It would be most agreeable to have your company. But it will be cold. You must wear your cape, and I will have another traveling rug brought for you."

Grandmama thanked her sincerely, and ten minutes later they were sitting side by side in the pony trap, with Agnes holding the reins. It was, as Agnes had warned, extremely cold. The wind had the kiss of ice on it. Clouds streamed in from the seaward side and the marsh grasses bent and rippled as if passed over by an unseen hand.

The trap was well sprung and the pony inexplicably enthusiastic, but it was still not the most comfortable ride. They left the village of Snave and moved quite quickly in what Grandmama presumed to be a westerly direction, and slightly south. It was all a matter of judging the wind and the smell of the sea. Agnes began by companionably telling her something about the village of Snargate and its inhabitants, and then explaining that from Snargate they would continue to Appledore. Then if there were time, to the Isle of Oxney as well, which of course was not an island at all, simply a rise from the flat land of the coast. However, if there were floods, then it would live up to its name.

Grandmama thought that possibly the history of these ancient villages might be quite interesting, but at present it was the history of the Barrington sisters that demanded her entire attention. She must direct Agnes to it, and not waste precious time, of which there was far too little as it was.

"You speak of the land so knowledgeably," she began with flattery. It always worked. "Your family has its roots here? You belong here?" People always wanted to belong. No one wished to be a stranger, as Maude must have been all her adult life.

"Oh, yes," Agnes said warmly. "My great-great-grandfather inherited the house and added to it a hundred and fifty years ago. It is Bedelia's of course. We had no brothers, unfortunately. And then it will be Randolph's. But then it would have been his anyway, because I have no sons either." She turned her face forward so Grandmama could see no more than a fleeting moment of her expression, and the moisture in her eyes could have been from the east wind. It was certainly cold enough.

"You are fortunate to have sisters," Grandmama told her. "I grew up with only brothers, and they were a great deal older than I. Too much so to be my friends."

"I'm sorry." There was no expression in Agnes's face, no lift of memory that made her smile.

Grandmama lied again. "You must have Christmas memories, and traditions in the family?" She looked at the baskets of jars covered with dainty cloth and tied with ribbons. "You do those so very well." More flattery, even if true.

"We always have," Agnes answered, still no lift in her voice.

Grandmama continued to probe, and finally drew a few more specific answers. In heaven's name, it was hard work! Did Pitt always have such a struggle? It was worse than pulling out teeth. But she was determined. Justice might depend upon this.

"I imagine you all did this together, when you were girls," she said with what she knew was tactlessness. "Or perhaps you were courting? I can think of nothing more romantic." Had she gone too far?

"Zachary did, with Bedelia," Agnes replied. "It was this season, and terribly cold. Several of the streams froze that year. I remember it." She remained looking forward, her expression bleak as the wind pulled strands of her hair loose and whipped them across her face.

Grandmama was momentarily lost. Zachary was Agnes's husband. She would dearly like to let this go. She heard pain in Agnes's voice, and old griefs were none of her affair. But Maude was dead. She could not feel the sting of salt in the air or see the wild flight of seabirds skittering down the wind and whirling back up again, high and wide, wheeling far out over the land.

"Mrs. Harcourt is very beautiful, even now," she tested the verbal knife. "She must have been quite breathtaking then. I have a distant relative who was like that."

"Yes." Agnes's hands were tight on the reins, the leather of her gloves strained. "Half the young men in the county were in love with her."

"And she chose Mr. Harcourt?" It was a stupid question, and probably entirely irrelevant to Maude's death, but she had nothing better to pursue.

"Yes." For a moment it seemed as if Agnes was going to say no more. Then she drew in her breath, wanting to speak after all. "Although it was not so simple as that."

"Really? I suppose things seldom are," Grandmama said sympathetically. "And even less often are they what they seem to be on the surface. People make very hasty judgments, sometimes."

"They are the easiest," Agnes agreed. She negotiated a sharp turn in the lane and Grandmama saw the village of Snargate ahead. This was proving very difficult indeed. They were almost at the village green. The inn, the church with ancient yew trees and graveyard, and the lych-gate covered with the bare vines of honeysuckle lay beyond.

They made their first delivery of Christmas fare, and the second, and then left Snargate and continued the short distance to Appledore.

"I suppose there is always speculation where there are sisters, and one is as beautiful as Bedelia," Grandmama said as soon as they were on their way again, blankets carefully tucked around shivering knees. The sky cleared a little and banners of blue appeared bright between the clouds.

As if deliberately hurting herself, Agnes told the story. "Maude didn't know about it, not really. She was away that Christmas. Aunt Josephine was ill and alone, and Maude went to look after her. Zachary was courting Bedelia. He was so in love with her. They went everywhere together, to the balls and the dinners and the theater in Dover, even through the snow. That was when the Queen was young and happy, and Prince Albert was so dashing. We saw drawings of them in the newspapers. It was before the Crimean War. I expect you remember?"

"I do." It had been a nightmare time. Her own husband had been alive, charming, persuasive, privately brutal, demanding things no decent woman ever imagined. She could still taste the wool of the carpet in her mouth and remember his weight on top of her, forcing her down. In public it had been all contentment, the glamour of endless crinoline skirts on a figure unrecognizable now in her too ample waist and hips. And at home a hell she could not think of without a hot shame making her feel sick. How could she, of all people, criticize anyone's cowardice? It stirred in her rage and pity, and a hunger to avenge it so sharp she could feel it. The bitter wind was almost a comfort.

But Agnes was lost in her own passions and did not even glance to see if her companion was with her mentally. "Then Arthur Harcourt arrived," she went on. "I think it was early March. The beginning of spring. The days were getting longer and everything was coming into bud. Arthur was not only handsome but charming and funny and kind. He could make us all laugh so hard we were embarrassed to be caught at it. One did not enjoy things so openly then. It was thought to be unladylike. He didn't care. And he could dance like an angel. Everything seemed worth doing when he was with us."

Grandmama thought she could guess the

rest. Bedelia fell out of love with Zachary and in love with Arthur, who was a much better catch. A far better catch. Poor Zachary was cast aside, and in time took second best, the duller, plainer Agnes. And Agnes accepted.

Without thinking, Grandmama reached across and put her hand on Agnes's where it rested above the edge of the rug, holding the reins tightly. She did not say anything. It was a silent understanding, a pity without words.

For a few moments they rode through the lanes toward Appledore in silence.

Then suddenly Agnes spoke again. "Of course we thought then that Bedelia and Arthur would marry. It seemed inevitable."

"Yes, it would," Grandmama agreed.

"But Aunt Josephine died, and Maude came back home. Everything changed," Agnes said.

"Indeed?" Grandmama had almost forgotten about Maude. "How?"

"Arthur and Maude just . . ." Agnes gave a tiny shrug. "Just seemed to . . . to fall so in love it was as if Bedelia ceased to exist. It didn't seem like a flirtation. Bedelia was . . . unable to believe it at first. I mean Maude, of all people? Goodness knows what she told him!"

"Told him?" Grandmama said before she could stop herself.

"Well, she must have told him something terrible about Bedelia to have caused him to abandon her like that! And of course untrue. Jealousy is . . . a very unkind thing. It eats the heart out of you, if you allow it to."

"Oh, that is true," Grandmama agreed sincerely. "It can be an instant passion, or a slow-growing one, but it is certainly deadly. But it seems as if Arthur saw through it, whatever it was." She hated saying that because it blamed Maude, and she was far from prepared to do that, but she must keep Agnes telling the story.

"Oh, yes," Agnes agreed. "It lasted perhaps a month, then Arthur came to his senses. He realized that he truly loved Bedelia. He broke off the silly business with Maude, and asked Bedelia to marry him. Of course she forgave him, and accepted."

"I see." She did not see at all.

Three sisters, two men. Someone had to have lost. Grandmama resented that it should have been Maude. Or had it really been all of them, no one truly finding what they hungered for? "And Maude?" she said quietly.

"Maude was heartbroken," Agnes replied,

her voice catching in her throat. She turned away as if there were something on the other side of the pony trap that required her attention, although there was nothing but the grasses and the sea wind and the marsh stretching out to the horizon. "She simply ran away. God knows where she went, but about a month later we received a postcard from Granada, in the south of Spain. There were only a few words on it. I remember. 'Going to Africa. Will probably stay. Maude.' "

And Bedelia had said she never wrote again. Was that true? "Until she returned a few days ago?" Grandmama asked aloud.

"That's right."

"Why did she come back, now, after all these years?"

Agnes shook her head and rubbed her hand over her eyes. "Perhaps she knew she was dying? Maybe she wanted to be buried here. People do. Want to be buried in their own land, I mean, their own earth."

"Did she say anything like that?"

"She did say something about death. I can't recall exactly what it was. But she was sad, that much was clear. I . . . I wish I had listened. My mind was on Lord Woollard's visit, and how anxious we all were that it should go well." Guilt was heavy in her voice and the misery of her face. "Arthur really does deserve recognition, you know. And the amount of good he could do with it would be enormous."

"And you were concerned that Maude's behavior would be inappropriate?"

Agnes glanced at Grandmama then away again, a mixture of impatience and shame in her face. "She had been living in extraordinary places for the last forty years, Mrs. Ellison. Places where people eat with their fingers, have no running water, where women do things that . . . I would rather not even think of, let alone speak about."

"I thought women in the Middle East were rather more modest than we are here in England," Grandmama said thoughtfully. "At least that was the impression I gained from Maude. They keep to their own apartments and don't speak to men other than those in their own families. Their clothing is certainly most decorous."

Agnes was frowning. "But Maude went unaccompanied, wandering around like a . . . like a man!" she exclaimed. "Who knows what happened to her? Her taste is highly questionable. Even her virtue, I'm afraid."

"I beg your pardon?" Grandmama said in angry disbelief, then realized she had gone too far. She must find an escape very quickly. "I'm so sorry," she apologized, the words all but choking her. "I felt so close to Maude because she confided in me, and I in her, that I am more offended than I have any right to be at the thought that someone who did not know her at all should question her virtue. It is quite unreasonable, and even impertinent of me. Please forgive me. She was your sister, not mine, and it is your right to defend her. I did not mean to presume." She watched Agnes's face intently, as if she were eager for pardon. She was actually extremely eager to see Agnes's reaction.

Agnes's hands froze on the reins and she stared ahead, even though they were now very close to the village of Appledore and she should have been slowing the pony.

"It is not presumptuous," she said, her face scarlet. Then she stopped again, still uncertain. "I'm sure you meant it only kindly. Perhaps we live too much in the past. Imagine too much."

"About Maude?" Grandmama had to ask. She was overwhelmingly aware of the misery in Agnes, and the knowledge that she would always be second choice. She was sorry for it — she even understood it — but it did not excuse lies, or answer justice now. They were passing the village church and she saw the festive wreaths on doors and a group of children ran past them shouting *Greetings!* What happens to people that they become bitter, and why do we not turn to each other, and help? We all walk a common path from cradle to grave, just stumble over different stones in it, trip in different holes, or drown in different puddles.

Agnes had not answered her.

"I understand," Grandmama said impulsively. "You had old memories of Maude once taking Arthur's affection, and you were afraid she would say or do something outrageous now. Perhaps even spoil his chances of receiving the peerage. So you made sure she could not be in the house when Lord Woollard was here. And now that she has died, you feel guilty, and of course it is too late to do anything about it."

Agnes turned to face her, eyes wide and hurt. She said nothing, but acknowledgment was as clear in her as if she had admitted it in so many words.

They delivered the jams and chutneys in Appledore and went on to the Isle of Oxney. The rising wind was cruelly cold. The horizon was blurred with gathering clouds and there was a smell of snow in the air. Perhaps it would not be necessary to feign a chill after all? Although how deep the snow would have to be to make travel inadvisable she did not know. St. Mary in the Marsh was only five miles away, not even an hour's journey. Maybe a few sneezes and a complaint of a sore throat would be better? She had barely scratched the surface of what there was to detect. There were emotions, old loves and jealousies, old wrongs, but what had caused them to erupt now? Pitt had said that there was always a reason why violence occurred at a particular time, some event that had sparked the final act.

Why had Maude come home? Why not before, in all the forty years of her exile? Or next year? Why at Christmas, not summer, when the weather would be infinitely more agreeable? Whose death was it that she had been referring to? Surely not her own?

On the ride back to Snave, she deliberately spoke only of Christmas arrangements. What to eat? Goose, naturally, and plenty of vegetables — roasted, boiled, baked, and with added sauces. After there would be a Christmas pudding rich with dried fruit and covered with brandied butter, and flamed at the time of serving. And covered with cream.

But before that there were literally dozens of other things to think of and prepare: cakes, pastries, mince pies, sweets, gingerbread, and all manner of drinks, both with and without alcohol. And naturally a wealth of decoration: wreaths and boughs, garlands, golden angels, colored bows, flowers made of silk and ribbon, pine cones painted with gold, little dolls to be given afterward to the poor of the village. There were presents to be made: skittles painted as wooden soldiers, pincushions, ornaments handmade and decorated with lace and beads and colored braid. The hours of work could hardly be counted. They spoke of them together, and remembered about their own childhood Christmases, before the advent of cards and trees and such modern ideas that so much added to the general happiness.

After luncheon Grandmama took a brief walk in the garden. She needed time alone to think. Detection required order in the mind. There were facts to be considered and weighed.

There was little to see beyond a well-tended neatness and very obvious architectural grace and skill. There were arbors, gravel walks, herbaceous borders carefully weeded, perennials cleared of dead foliage, a flight of steps that curved up to a pergola covered with the skeletons of roses, and finally a less formal woodland overlooking the open marsh.

It was very wet underfoot, and rather muddy. The long grasses soaked the hem of her skirt, but it was inevitable. In spring this would be beautiful with flowers: snow-drops, primroses in all likelihood, wood anemones, certainly bluebells, wild daisies, campion. Perhaps narcissi with their piercingly sweet scent. She saw two or three crowns of foxglove leaves. She loved their elegant spires in purples or white. One of them looked a little ragged, as if an animal had cropped it. Except that no animal would eat foxglove — it was poisonous. Creatures always seemed to know. It slowed the heart. It was used by doctors for people whose hearts raced. Digitalis. She froze. Raced . . . slowed. Stopped!

Was that it? The answer she was searching for? She bent and looked at the leaves again. There was no earthly way of proving it, but she was perfectly sure someone had picked two or three leaves. The broken ends were visible.

She stood up again slowly. How could she find out who? It must have been the day Maude was here. Had it been wet or dry? Never dry in winter in this wood, but if freezing then the ice would prevent anyone getting as wet as she was now, or as muddy.

Four days before, Joshua had received Bedelia's letter. Think! Windy, the noise of it howling in the eaves was clear in her mind. It had irritated her unbearably. And relatively mild. Who had come in with muddy boots, a dress soaked at the hems? A ladies' maid would know. But how to ask her?

She turned and walked briskly back into the house and went to find Mrs. Ward.

"I'm so sorry," she apologized profusely; startled that she meant it without any pretense at all. "I went walking in the garden and became distracted with the beauty of it."

"It is lovely, isn't it," Mrs. Ward agreed. "That's Mrs. Harcourt's skill. Mrs. Sullivan can paint a picture of a flower that's both lovely and correct, but it's Mrs. Harcourt who plans the garden itself."

"What a gift," Grandmama said. "And one from which we all benefit. But I am afraid that I have thoroughly muddied both my boots, and the hem of your dress. It was deeply careless of me, and I regret it now."

"Oh, don't worry! It happens all the time!" Mrs. Ward dismissed it. "Your own dress is quite clean and dry, and Nora can clean this again in no time."

"I'm sure it doesn't happen to everybody,"

119

Grandmama told her. "I cannot imagine Mrs. Harcourt being so inelegant, or so thoughtless. You cannot name me the last time she did this!"

Mrs. Ward smiled. "Certainly I can! The very day Miss Maude came home. Went looking for some nice branches to add to the flowers in the hall. Woodland branches can be most graceful in a vase. Please don't think of it, Mrs. Ellison."

"Really?" Grandmama's heart was racing. So it was Bedelia. But she should be certain. "I expect she and Clara were in quite a state, with Lord Woollard expected as well."

"Certainly. She also went out on an errand and came back as muddy as you like. Poor Nora was beside herself. Then Mrs. Sullivan the day after. At least I think it was. I'll find Nora and send her up to you."

"Thank you. You are most considerate." Grandmama left with her mind whirling. So who had boiled up the leaves? Where? How could she find that out? Perhaps they were simply crushed and steeped, as one makes a cup of tea! That could have been any of them. She must think more — pay attention. And be careful!

In the afternoon Grandmama offered to help Bedelia in some of the last-minute preparations. Of course Cook would see to the meal itself, and most of the other things that required the use of the kitchen. But there was still much sewing to be done, lavender bags that were not finished, ornamental roses to be made, and definitely more decorations for the great tree in the hall.

"I could have sworn that we had more than this last year!" Bedelia said, looking at it with dismay. "It seems almost bare, don't you think, Mrs. Ellison?"

Grandmama regarded the huge tree, its dark green needles still fresh and scented with earth and pine. It was liberally decorated with ribbons and ornaments, and there was a handsome pile of parcels beneath, and smaller ones with lace and flowers hanging from the branches. It was far from bare, but certainly there were places where more could be hung. It was important that she make herself necessary.

"It is very handsome," she answered judiciously. "But you are quite right, of course. There are still one or two places to be filled in. I am sure it would not be difficult to find the materials to make a couple of dozen more ornaments. One needs only a child's ball, perhaps two of different sizes would be even better, paste, and as many different colors of paper as possible, beads, dried flowers, ribbon, lace, whatever else can be spared that is pretty. Sometimes an old gown can provide an amazing variety of bits and pieces. It's not difficult to make tiny dolls, or angels." She had rather run away with herself, but it was all in the growingly desperate cause of detection. Very definite ideas were crystallizing in her mind, but she needed more time!

Christmas was supposed to be a time of forgiveness, but surely there could be no healing without honor, no real peace without change of heart? And no change without truth.

"It is not a lack of materials," Bedelia told her. "I have not the time, and I doubt the maids have the skill."

"I should be happy to help you, if I may?" Grandmama offered. She had not been so courteous in years, and in spite of her amusement at herself, she was rather enjoying it. It was like a step outside her own life, a curious freedom from the expectations of others, or the chains of past failure.

"I should be delighted to contribute something to such a glorious tree," she continued eagerly. "And also a sort of family tradition. The Barringtons have been in this village for so many generations there are bound to be scores of people who will call in to wish you season's greetings and share your hospitality." That was certain. Tradesmen always paid their respects this time of year and partook of mince pies, candied fruit and nuts, and of course a cup of punch.

Bedelia accepted, and half an hour later they were sitting in the sewing room at opposite sides of the table cannibalizing an old evening gown, cutting off beads, braid, fine silk and velvet pieces, and the paler ribbons and lace from two old petticoats that had also been found.

"There is too much dark red," Bedelia said critically. "All of the silk and velvet is the same shade."

"That is true," Grandmama agreed. "What we really need is something else bright in a completely different tone." She looked at Bedelia with a frown. "I have a very daring idea. Perhaps you would find it offensive, but I have to ask. If it grieves you, I apologize in advance."

"Good gracious!" Bedelia was intrigued. "I am not easily shocked. What is this idea?"

"Maude said that she traveled in many strange and exotic places."

A faint distaste flashed in Bedelia's eyes but she masked it. "Is that helpful?"

"No doubt she wore some . . . strange clothes," Grandmama said tentatively. "Possibly of colors we would not choose."

Bedelia understood instantly and her face lit with pleasure.

"Oh! But of course! How clever of you. Yes, certainly, some of them might be cut up for the most excellent Christmas ornaments."

Grandmama felt a chill at the thought of cutting up any of Maude's clothes, things she had worn in the places that she had obviously loved so far from home. She might have stood in the sunset in some Persian garden and smelled the perfume of strange trees and the wind off the desert and looked up to unimaginable stars. Or perhaps there would be scarves of silk she had bought at a noisy, multitudinous bazaar in Marrakech, or some such city. They should all be treated with tenderness, folded to keep in the odor of spices and strange fruit, oils and leathers, and the smoke from the campfires.

"You are so clever, Mrs. Ellison," Bedelia was saying. "Of course most of her things are here and we have only to unpack them. And it is unlikely that any of them are things that anyone else would wear. I really do not care to offer them, even to the poor. It would be . . ."

"Disrespectful," Grandmama filled in, meaning it, and enjoying forcing Bedelia to agree. She hated herself for doing it, but truth required some strange sacrifices. "This way they will be totally anonymous, and give pleasure for years to come." Forgive me, Maude, she thought to herself. Detection is not easy, and I refuse to fail. She stood up. "I suppose we should begin. See what we can find." That was crass. She had not been invited to look into Maude's effects, but she was most curious to see if there was anything helpful. No one else who knew that she had been murdered would ever have such an opportunity.

If Bedelia were offended she did not show it.

Upstairs in the box room, where the luggage had been stored, they set about opening the two trunks Maude had brought back with her. Grandmama found herself with the one packed with ordinary blouses and skirts, underclothes, and sensible, rather scuffed boots. They were of moderate quality linen, cotton, and some of raw, unbleached wool. She wondered in what marvelous places Maude had worn these. What had she seen, what emotions of joy, pain, or loneliness had she felt? Had she longed for home, or had she been at home wherever she was, with friends, even people who loved her?

She glanced across at Bedelia and studied her face as she pulled out a length of silk striped in purples, scarlets, crimsons, and tawny golds mingled with a hot pink. She drew in her breath sharply. At first it seemed to be pleasure, excitement, even a kind of longing. Then her mouth hardened and there was hurt in her eyes.

"Good heavens above!" she said sharply. "What on earth could she have worn this for? Whatever is it?" She shook it out until it billowed and appeared to be a sheet with very little distinctive shape. "One can only hope it was a gift, and not something she purchased for herself. No woman could wear such a thing, even at twenty, never mind at Maude's age! She would have looked like something out of the circus!" She started to laugh, then stopped abruptly. "A very good thing we looked at this first, Mrs. Ellison. If the servants had seen it we should be the talk of the village."

Grandmama felt her fury flare up and if she had dared she would have lashed out verbally in Maude's defense. But there were bigger considerations, and with intense difficulty she choked back the words. She forced herself to look as close to good-natured as she could manage, which effort cost her dearly. "Instead they will be talking about the gorgeous and perfectly unique ornaments on your tree," she said sweetly. "And you will be able to say that they are a remembrance of your sister."

Bedelia sat rigid, her eyes unmoving, her face set. It could have been grief, or the complexity and hurt of any memory, including anger that would never now be redeemed, or regret for forgiveness too late. Or even debts uncollected. The only thing Grandmama was certain of was that the emotion was deep, and that it brought no ease or pleasure.

They took the silks downstairs and Bedelia cut into them with large fabric shears. Bright clouds like desert sunsets drifted across the table and onto the floor. Grandmama picked them up and began to work on the papier-mâché and paste to make the basic balls before they should be covered in the bright gauze. After that they would stitch little dolls to dress in the gold and bronze and white with pearls. She smiled at the prospect. It was fun to create beauty.

But she was not here to enjoy herself. This silk in her hands had been a wonderful, wild, garish robe that Maude had worn on the hot roads of Arabia, or somewhere like it.

"I imagine Maude must have known some very different people," she said thoughtfully. "They would seem odd to us, perhaps even frightening." She allowed the lamplight to fall on the purple silk and the brazen red. "I cannot imagine wearing these colors together."

"Nor could anyone else outside a fairground!" Bedelia responded. "You see why we could not have her here when Lord Woollard stayed. We allowed him the courtesy of not shocking or embarrassing him."

"Is he a man of small experience?" Grandmama inquired with as much innocence as she could contrive.

"Of discreet taste and excellent family," Bedelia said coolly. "His wife, whom I have met, is the sister of one of Her Majesty's ladies-in-waiting. An excellent person."

Perhaps even a week ago Grandmama would have been impressed. Now all she could think of was Maude's Persian garden with the small owls in the dusk.

There was a knock on the door and Agnes came in. A brief conversation followed about parties, games to be played, especially blindman's bluff, and of course refreshments.

"We must remember some lemon curd tarts for Mrs. Hethersett," Agnes reminded her. "She is always so fond of them."

"She will have to make her own," Bedelia responded. "She will not be coming."

"Oh, dear! Is she unwell again?" Agnes asked sympathetically.

"She will not be coming because I have not invited her," Bedelia said tersely. "She was unforgivably rude."

"That was over a year ago!" Agnes protested.

"It was," Bedelia agreed. "What has that to do with it?"

Agnes did not argue. She admired the rapidly progressing baubles, and returned to the task of organizing pies and tarts.

"How very unpleasant," Grandmama sympathized, wondering what on earth Mrs. Hethersett could have said that Bedelia still bore a grudge a year later, and at Christmas, of all times. "She must have been dreadfully rude to distress you so much." She nearly added that she could not understand why people should be rude, but that was too big a lie to swallow. She could understand rudeness perfectly, and practice it to the level of an art. It was something she had never previously been ashamed of, but now it was oddly distasteful to her.

"She imagines I will forget," Bedelia responded. "But she is quite mistaken, as she will learn."

Grandmama bent to the stitching again, blending the bright colors with less pleasure, and wondered what Maude had done to Bedelia that old memories lingered so long in unforgiveness.

Why had Maude returned now? Was it possible Grandmama was completely mistaken? Had she allowed her bored and lonely imagination to conjure up murder where there was only an unexpected death, and grief that looked like anger? And a proud woman who would not allow another to see that she was bitterly ashamed of having turned away her sister for fear that her behavior was socially inappropriate, and now regretted it so terribly when it was too late? Was Grandmama making a crime out of what was only a tragedy?

Dinner was tense again. As on the first night there was the palpable undercurrent of emotions that perhaps there always is in families: knowledge of weaknesses, indulgences, things said that would have been better forgotten, only there is always someone who will remind.

Aloud they recalled past Christmases,

particularly those when Randolph had been a boy, which necessarily excluded Clara. Grandmama studied her face and saw the flicker of hurt in it, and then of annoyance.

The others were enjoying themselves. For once Arthur joined in the laughter and the open affection as Bedelia told a tale of Randolph's surprise at receiving a set of tin soldiers in perfect replica of Wellington's army at Waterloo. It seemed he had refused to come to the table, even for goose. He was so enraptured he could not put his soldiers down. Bedelia had tried to insist, but Arthur had said it was Christmas, and Randolph should do as he pleased.

Grandmama found herself smiling also — until she saw the hunger in Zachary's eyes, his look at Bedelia, Agnes's look at him, and remembered that Randolph was the only one among all four of them likely to have a child. He was forty. Clara, strong-willed and ambitious, was a great deal younger. When would they have children? Or might that be another grief waiting in the wings?

She would have liked to have had more children herself; a daughter like Charlotte might have made all the difference, or even like Emily. A lot of work, a lot of frustration and disappointment, but who could measure the happiness?

It would be better if she did not think of the past anymore. Far better to treasure what you have than grieve over what you have not.

She looked around their faces again. Why does anybody hate someone enough to kill them, with all the risk involved? You don't, if you are sane. You kill to protect, to keep what you have and love: position, power, money, even safety from scandal, the pain of humiliation, or loss, or the terror in loneliness. She could easily imagine that. Perhaps we were all as fragile, if one found the right passion, the fear that eats at the soul.

She looked at the light from the chandeliers glittering on the silver, the crystal, at the white linen, the lilies from the hothouse, and the red wine, all the different faces, and wondered if she really wanted to know the answer.

Then she remembered Maude's laughter, and the memories in her eyes as she described the moonlight over the desert. There was no escaping the answer. That would be the ultimate, irredeemable cowardice.

The following day the scullery maid cut her finger so badly she could not use her hand,

and the kitchen was in pandemonium. Agnes had been going to take the pony trap to deliver gifts to the vicar's widow in Dymchurch, and now all plans had to be rearranged.

Without a thought for her own competence for such a task, Grandmama offered to go in her stead. The stable boy could drive her and she would call, with explanations, upon Mrs. Dowson and give her the already wrapped gifts for herself, and one or two other families.

Her offer was accepted, and at ten o'clock they set off, she feeling very pleased with herself. It was a bitter day with clouds piling slate gray on the horizon, and the wind had veered round to come from the north with ice on the edge.

Grandmama sat with the rug wrapped tightly around her knees and tucked in under her, hoping profoundly that it would not snow before she returned to Snave, or she might find that the chill she had considered pretending could be only too real. She had no desire whatever to spend Christmas in bed with a fever!

And then another thought assailed her, even more unpleasant. What if she discovered beyond doubt who it was that had picked the foxglove leaves and distilled their poison, and could prove it? And that person became aware of the fact! Then it might be a great deal more than a chill that afflicted her. She wondered if it was painful to die of a heart slowing until it stopped altogether. She could feel it bumping in her chest now with fear.

If she died, would anyone miss her enough to be sorry? Would anyone's world be colder or grayer because she was not in it?

She thought of Maude alone in the house of strangers who had taken her in out of kindness, or worse, a sense of duty. Or pity? That was even worse again. Had Maude felt obliged to work hard to be charming, hide the rejection she must feel inside in order to win their warmth? Had she even known that Grandmama liked her, genuinely liked her?

Now, that was a lie. Her face was hot in spite of the knife-edge wind. She had loathed Maude, even before she arrived, because Maude would displace her as the center of attention. She had realized only after Maude was dead how much she had liked her, admired her, found her exciting to listen to, freeing the imagination and awakening dreams. She wished now with a desire so strong it was like a physical ache that she had allowed Maude to see that she

134

liked her, more than anyone else she could think of.

They were going toward the sea and she could smell the salt more sharply. Dymchurch was not far from St. Mary in the Marsh. She could not return home until she had solved this. It would be a betrayal not only of Maude, but of friendship itself. The length of it was irrelevant, it was the depth that mattered.

She ignored the great ragged skies, clouds streaming across its vastness like the torn banners of an army, spears of ice not far behind. As they drove into the village itself she could hear the roaring of the surf on the shore and the tower of the church seemed to stand aloft against the racing darkness coming in on the storm.

They pulled up to a small cottage with bare vines covering the arch over the gate and the stable boy announced that they had arrived. He said he would take the parcels in for her, as soon as they had ascertained that Mrs. Dowson was at home. Then he would take the pony and trap around to the stable to shelter until she was ready to leave again. He looked anxiously at the sky, and then smiled, showing gapped teeth.

Grandmama thanked him and with his help alighted.

Mrs. Dowson was at home. She was a lean woman with narrow shoulders and bright eyes. She must have been closer to eighty than seventy, but seemed to be still in excellent health. There was a color in her cheeks as if she had recently been outside, even in this darkening weather.

Grandmama introduced herself.

"My name is Mariah Ellison, Mrs. Dowson. Please excuse me for calling unannounced on Mrs. Harcourt's behalf, but I am afraid I have accepted their hospitality in the wake of tragedy, and the whole family is bravely making the very best of a hard situation. I offered to come on this errand for her. I feel it is the least I can do."

"Oh, dear. I'm so sorry. Very kind of you, Mrs. Ellison." She looked at Grandmama curiously but without apprehension. "May I offer you tea, and perhaps a mince pie or something of the sort?" She did not ask what the tragedy had been. Was that extreme discretion, or had word somehow come this far already?

"Thank you," Grandmama accepted, wondering if there were a third possibility, that she simply did not care. "I admit, it is remarkably cold outside. I do not know this area very well. I live in London and am merely visiting, but I find something most pleasing about the sea air, even when there is so very much of it."

Mrs. Dowson smiled. "It pleases me, too," she agreed, conducting the way into a small but very pretty sitting room. It was low-ceilinged, with furniture covered in floral chintz, and a fire burning in the hearth. She rang the bell, and when the maid came, requested tea and tarts.

"Now, my dear," she said when they were seated, "what is the trouble with poor Agnes now? I imagine it is Agnes, is it not?"

How interesting, Grandmama thought. Aloud she said, "I am afraid it is all of them. Did you ever know the third sister, Miss Maude Barrington?"

Something hardened in Mrs. Dowson's face, and her eyes were chill. "I did. But if you have come to say something uncomplimentary about her, I would thank you not to. I know she was a little unruly, and perhaps she threw herself too fully into things, but she had a good heart, and it was all very long ago. I think one should take one's victories very lightly, and one's losses with silence and dignity, do you not agree, Mrs. Ellison?"

How curious! Not at all what Grandmama had expected. Mrs. Dowson's eyes might be bright and cold, but they kindled a sudden new warmth in Grandmama's mind.

"Indeed I do," she said heartily. "That is one of the reasons I felt an affection for Maude the moment I met her. It is one of the great sadnesses of my life that I knew her such a very short time."

"I beg your pardon?" Mrs. Dowson said huskily, her face now filled with alarm.

Even a week ago Grandmama would have made a condescending reply to that. Now all she wanted to do was find some kinder way of telling the news.

"I am so sorry. Maude arrived home from abroad and because of other family commitments at her sister's house, she came and stayed with her cousin, Mr. Joshua Fielding, who is also a relative of mine, hence my presence there. Maude died, quite peacefully in her sleep, three days ago." She saw the undisguised pain in the old lady's face. "I felt so very grieved I chose to take the news to her family in person, rather than merely send some written message," she concluded, "which is how I come to be still staying with them now. I am doing what little I can to help."

"Oh, dear," Mrs. Dowson said, shaking her head a little. "I assumed it was no more than another of Agnes's chills, or whatever it is she has. How stupid of me. One should not assume. This is a deep loss." Suddenly the tears filled her eyes. "I'm so sorry," she apologized.

Grandmama did not find it absurd that after forty years Mrs. Dowson should still grieve so keenly. Time does not cloud certain memories. Bright days from youth, laughter and friendship can remain.

But crass as it seemed, it was also an opportunity that she could not afford to ignore. "Did you know her well, before she left to travel abroad?" she asked.

"Oh yes," Mrs. Dowson smiled. "I knew all the girls then. My husband was a curate, just young in his ministry. Very earnest, you know, as dedicated men can be. I rather think Maude overwhelmed him. She was so fierce in her love for Arthur Harcourt. And of course Arthur was quite the dashing young man-about-town. He was extraordinarily handsome, and he knew it. But he could hardly fail to. If he'd crooked a finger at any of the girls in the south of England they'd have followed him. I might have myself, if I'd thought he meant it. But I was never very pretty, and I was happy enough with Walter. He was genuine. I rather thought Arthur wasn't."

"Sincere? Was he simply playing with Maude?"

Suddenly Grandmama's liking for Arthur Harcourt evaporated as if she had torn the smiling mask off and seen rotten flesh underneath.

"Oh no," Mrs. Dowson said quickly. "That was where Walter and I disagreed. He thought Arthur loved Bedelia. He called them a perfect match. Something of an idealist, my husband. Thought beauty was bone deep, not just a chance of coloring and half an inch here and there, and of course confidence. Self-belief, you know? Imagine how the map of the world might have been changed if Cleopatra's nose had been half an inch longer! Then Caesar might not have fallen in love with her, or Mark Anthony either."

Grandmama was carried along in a hurricane of thought.

"I'm so sorry," Mrs. Dowson apologized again. "Walter always said my mind was totally undisciplined. I told him that was not so at all, simply that it moved in a different pattern from his. Bedelia Barrington could twist him around her little finger! And half the men in the county, too. Poor Zachary never got over it, which is such a shame. Agnes was the better girl, if only she could have believed that herself!"

Grandmama did not interrupt her. The

tea arrived. Mrs. Dowson poured, and passed the mince pie and jam tarts.

"Bedelia thought she was glamorous, Agnes was dull, and Maude was plain and eccentric. Because of her confidence, far too many people believed that she must be right."

"But she was not . . ."

"Certainly she was," Mrs. Dowson contradicted her. "But only because we allowed her to be. Except Maude. She knew Bedelia's beauty was of no real value. No warmth in it, do you see?"

"But she fell in love with Arthur? So much so that she could not bear it when he came to his senses and married Bedelia after all?" Grandmama deliberately chose her words provocatively.

"I used to think he lost his senses again," Mrs. Dowson argued. "I was furious with Maude for not fighting for the man she loved. Fancy simply giving up and running away like that! Off to North Africa, and then Egypt and Persia. Riding horses in the desert, and camels too, for all I can say. Lived in tents and gave what was left of her heart to the Persians."

"She wrote to you!" Grandmama was astonished, and delighted. Maude had had a friend here who had cared for her over the years and kept her in touch with home.

"Of course," Mrs. Dowson said indignantly. "She never told me why she left, but I came to realize it was a matter of honor, and must not ever be discussed. She did what she believed to be the right thing. But I don't think that she ever stopped loving Arthur."

New ideas began to form in Grandmama's mind. "Mrs. Dowson, do you know why Maude chose to come home now, after so long?" she asked. "Did she have any . . . any anxieties about her health?"

"Not that she confided in me." Mrs. Dowson frowned. "She was certainly afraid, a little oppressed by the thought of returning after so long. But the gentleman she had cared for in Persia, and who had loved her, had died. She told me that. It grieved her very much, and it also meant that she had no reason for remaining there anymore. In fact she implied that without his protection it would be unwise for her to do so. I do not know their relationship. I never asked and she never told me, but it was not regular, as you and I would use the term."

"I see. Was Bedelia aware of this?" Was that the scandal she was afraid might come to Lord Woollard's ears — even perhaps quite frankly told by Maude, in order to shock? After Bedelia's coolness over the years, and the fact that it was she Arthur had married, whatever his reason, it would not be unnatural now if Maude had been unable to resist at least preventing her sister from becoming Lady Harcourt. She asked Mrs. Dowson as much.

"She may have been tempted," Mrs. Dowson replied. "But she would not have done it. Maude never bore a grudge. That was Bedelia."

"Was Bedelia not very much in love with Arthur, even before Maude returned from caring for her aunt?" Grandmama asked.

"Maude did tell you a great deal, didn't she?" Mrs. Dowson observed.

Grandmama merely smiled.

"However much Maude had despised Bedelia, she would never have hurt Arthur," Mrs. Dowson continued. "As I said, she never stopped loving him. And I refer to that emotion that seeks the best for the other, the honor and happiness and inward spiritual journey; not the hunger to possess at all costs, the joy for oneself in their company and the feeling that they are happy only when they are with you. That is Bedelia, all about winning. And poor Agnes was concerned she was always going to be no more than second-best."

"Then why was Arthur so foolish?" Grandmama marveled. "Was he really blinded by mere physical . . . oh." A far simpler and more understandable answer came to her mind. She saw that Mrs. Dowson was watching her intently. She felt the heat in her cheeks as if Mrs. Dowson could read her thoughts.

"I do not know," Mrs. Dowson said quietly. "But I believe Maude did, and that is why Bedelia was very happy that she should remain in Persia for the rest of her life."

The idea became firmer in Grandmama's mind. It made sense of what was otherwise outside the character and nature of the people she had observed. Looking at Mrs. Dowson, she was certain she had guessed the same answer. She smiled across at her. "How very sad," she said gently, aware of what an absurd understatement that was. "Poor Arthur." She hesitated. "And poor Zachary."

"And Agnes," Mrs. Dowson added. "But above all, I wish that Maude had not . . . not suffered so."

"But she made the best of it," Grandmama said with an intensity of feeling, an absolute conviction that welled up inside her, driving away all doubt.

Mrs. Dowson nodded. "Maude always

knew how to live. She knew the worst was there and she accepted the pain as part of the truth of things, but she chose to see the best also, and to find the joy in variety. She did not close herself off from the richness of experience. I think that was her gift. I shall miss her terribly."

"Even though I knew her only briefly, I shall miss her also," Grandmama confessed. "But I am profoundly grateful that I did know her. And . . . and gratitude is something I have not felt lately. Simply to have that back is a . . ." She did not know how to finish. She sniffed, pulled her emotions together with an effort, then rose to her feet. "But I have something to do. I must return to Snave and attend to it. Thank you very much for your hospitality, Mrs. Dowson, and even more for the understanding you have given me. May I wish you the joy of the season, and remembrance of all that is good in the past, together with hope for the future."

Mrs. Dowson rose also. "Why, how graciously put, Mrs. Ellison. I shall endeavor to remember that. May I wish you joy also, and safety in your journey, both in the body and in the spirit? Happy Christmas."

Outside it was beginning to snow, white flurries on the wind. So far it was only dusting the ground, but the heavy pall of cloud to the north made it apparent that there was a great deal more to come. Whether she wanted to or not, Grandmama would be unlikely to be able to return to St. Mary in the Marsh today. That was a good thing. What she had to do would be best done in the evening, when they were all together after dinner. It would be uncomfortable, extremely so. She felt a sinking in her stomach as she sat in the pony trap, wrapped against the snow. The biting wind was behind her and the roar of the sea breaking on the shore growing fainter as they moved inland between the wide, flat fields, beginning to whiten.

She was afraid. She admitted it to herself. She was afraid of unpleasantness, even physical attack, although she expected any attack to be secret, disguised as the one on Maude had been. Even more than that, and it surprised her, she was afraid of not doing it well.

But then, like Agnes, she had regarded herself as a failure most of her life. She had lived a lie, always pretending to be a highly respectable woman, even aggressively so, married to a man who had died relatively young and left her grieving since her late forties, unable to recover from the loss.

In truth, she had married wretchedly, and his death had released her, at least on the outside. She had never allowed herself to be released in her own mind, and worse still, in her heart. She had kept up the lie, to save her pride.

Of course no one ever needed to know the details, but she could have been honest with herself, and it would slowly have spread through her manner, her beliefs, and in the end the way she had seen and been seen by others.

Maude Barrington had suffered a monstrous injustice. She had borne it apparently without bitterness. If it had marred an earlier part of her life, perhaps when she first went abroad, she had healed her own spirit from the damage and gone on to live a passionate and adventurous life. Perhaps it had never been comfortable, but what was comfort worth? Bitterness, blame, and self-hatred were never comfortable either. And perhaps they were also not as safe as she had once imagined. They were a slow-growing disease within, killing inch by inch.

It was snowing quite hard now, lying thick and light on the ground, beginning to drift on the windward side of the furrows left in the fields after their winter plowing, and on the trunks of the trees. The wind was blow-ing too hard for the snow to stay on the branches as they swayed against the sky. There was little sound from the pony's hooves because the ground was blanketed already, just the deep moan of the wind and the creak of the wheels. It was a hard, beautiful world, invigorating, ice-cold, and on every side, sweet and sharp-smelling from the sea, infinitely wide.

She arrived back at Snave before she was really ready, but there was no help for it. And maybe she would never feel as if it were time. She allowed the stable boy to assist her, and to his surprise thanked him for his care.

Inside she took off her cape and shawl and was very glad to be in the warmth again. Her hands were almost numb from the cold and her face was stinging, her eyes watering, but she had never felt more intensely alive. She was terrified, and yet there was an unmistakable bubble of courage inside her, as if something of Maude's vitality and hunger for life had been bequeathed to her.

She was too late for luncheon, and too excited to eat much anyway. Cook had prepared a tray for her with soup and new, warm bread, and that was really all she required. She thanked her sincerely, with a compliment, and after finishing it all, went upstairs with the excuse that she wished to lie down. In reality she wanted to prepare herself for the evening. It was going to be one of the biggest of her life, perhaps her only real achievement. It would require all the nerve and the intelligence she possessed. There was in her mind no doubt of the truth now. Proving it would be altogether another matter, but if she did not attempt it, whatever it cost her, then she would have failed the last chance that fate had offered.

She dressed very carefully, in the housekeeper's best black gown, and thanked the maid. It seemed appropriate. She was going to be a different person from the woman she had been as long as she could clearly remember. She was going to be brave, face all the ugliness, the shame, and the failure, and be gentle toward them, because she understood them intimately. She had been a liar herself, and every stupid ugly corner of it was familiar. She had been a coward, and its corroding shroud had covered every part of her life. She had tried to touch other people's lives with her own meanness of spirit, her belief in failure. There was no victory in that. One could spoil others, dirty them, damage what could have been whole. Now she could touch all their wounds with pity, but none of them could deceive her.

She regarded herself in the glass. She looked different from the way she was accustomed. It was more than the dress that was not her own; the face also was not the one that had been hers for so long. There was color in her skin. Her eyes were brighter. Most of all the sulk had gone from her lips, and the lines seemed to be curving upward, not down.

Ridiculous! She had never been pretty, and she wasn't now. If she did not know better, she would think she had been imbibing rather too freely of the Christmas spirit, of that nature that comes in a bottle!

She straightened her skirt a last time, and went down to join the family for dinner. Tomorrow she would leave. She would probably have to, even if the snow were up to the eaves! There was something exhilarating, and a little mad, in casting the last die, crossing the Rubicon, if she were remembering her schoolroom history correctly. It was war! Triumph or disaster, because she could not stop until it was over.

■ ■ ■ ■

PART THREE

■ ■ ■ ■

She was a few minutes late, as she had intended. There was very little time before dinner was announced and they all went into the dining room. It was now looking even more festive, with scarlet berries intertwined in the wreaths and the swags along the mantelpiece, all tied with gold ribbons. There were scarlet candles on the table, even though they were not yet lit, and everything seemed to be touched with light from the chandeliers.

"I hope you are recovered from your journey, Mrs. Ellison?" Arthur asked with concern. "I'm afraid the weather turned most unpleasant before you were able to return."

"I should not have allowed you to go," Bedelia added. "I had not realized it would take you so long."

"It was entirely my own fault," Grandmama replied. "I could have been back earlier, and I should have, for the stable boy's and the pony's sake, if nothing else. To tell you the truth, the ride back was very beautiful. I have not been out in a snowstorm for so long that I had forgotten how amazing it is. The sense of the power and magnitude of nature is very marvelous."

"What a refreshing view," Arthur said, then suddenly the sadness filled his eyes, overwhelming him. "You remind me of Maude." He stopped, unable to continue.

It was the greatest compliment Grandmama had ever received, but she could not afford to stop and savor it now.

She continued with what she had intended to say, regardless of their responses. She even ignored the butler and the footman serving the soup.

"Thank you, Mr. Harcourt. The more I learn of Maude, the more I appreciate how very much that means. I know that for you it is as profound as it could be, and I wish more than you can be aware of to live up to it."

Bedelia was startled, then her mouth curled in a smile more of disdain than amusement. "We all grieve for Maude, Mrs. Ellison, but there is no requirement for you to cater to our family perception with such praise." She left the implied adjective "fulsome" unsaid, but it hung in the air.

"Oh, I'm not!" Grandmama said candidly, her eyes wide. "Maude was a most remarkable person. I learned far more of just how amazing from Mrs. Dowson. That, I'm afraid, is why I stayed so long."

Bedelia was stiff, her shoulders like carved ivory beneath her violet taffeta gown. "Mrs. Dowson is sentimental," she replied coolly. "A vicar's widow and obliged to see the best in people."

"Perhaps the vicar did," Grandmama corrected her. "Mrs. Dowson certainly does not. She is quite capable of seeing pride, greed, selfishness, and other things; cowardice in particular." She smiled at Agnes. "The acceptance of failure because one does not have the courage to face what one is afraid of, and pay the price in comfort that is sometimes necessary for success."

The blood drained from Agnes's face, leaving her ashen. Her spoon slithered into her soup dish and she ignored it.

Zachary started to speak, and then choked on whatever it was he had been going to say.

It was Randolph who came to her rescue. "That sounds extremely harsh, Mrs. Ellison. How on earth would Mrs. Dowson be in a position to know anything of that sort about anybody? And what she did know must have come to her in a privileged position, and therefore should not be repeated."

"Most un-Christian," Clara added.

"It can be very difficult to recognize the right thing to do, at times," Grandmama continued, grateful for the extraordinary ease with which the opportunities she needed were opening up for her. "But I must not misrepresent Mrs. Dowson. Actually she said nothing, except to praise Maude's love of beauty, her laughter, and above all her courage to make the best of her life, even after so great a sacrifice, which was given silently and with the utmost dignity."

Zachary looked totally confused. Arthur was pale, his breathing seemed painful. Bedelia was as white as Agnes now and her hands on her lap were clenched. No one ate.

"I am not sure what you imagine you are referring to, Mrs. Ellison," she said icily. "It appears you are a lonely woman with nothing to do, and you have concerned yourself in our family's affairs in a way that exceeds even your imagined duty to Maude, whom you barely met. Your meddlesomeness has run away with you. I think we had better find a way to return you to St. Mary in the

Marsh tomorrow, regardless of the weather. I am sure that would be better for all of us."

Randolph blushed scarlet.

It was Arthur who spoke. "Bedelia, that is unnecessary. I apologize, Mrs. Ellison. I don't know what Maude told you, but I think you must have misunderstood her."

"She told me nothing," Grandmama said, meeting his eyes. "She would never betray you like that! And surely by now you must know beyond any question at all that she would not betray Bedelia either! She did not come here to cause any kind of trouble. The man who had loved her and protected her in Persia died, and she could no longer remain there. She came back home because she wished to. Perhaps she even imagined that after all these years she would be welcome. Which of course was an error. Quite obviously she was not."

"You have no right to say that!" Clara cut in. "She had been living in the desert, in tents and by campfires, like a . . . a gypsy! And with a foreign man to whom she was not married! We could hardly have her in the house at the same time as Lord Woollard! My father-in-law has given more to society than you have any idea. This peerage would have been not only a just reward but an opportunity to do even more good.

We could not jeopardize that!"

"And it would, in time, have made you Lady Harcourt," Grandmama added. "With all that that means. Of course you did not wish to lose such a prize."

"Oh, no . . . I . . ." Clara faded into silence. She had the grace to be ashamed.

"Stuff and nonsense!" Bedelia snapped. "You overstep yourself, Mrs. Ellison. Your behavior is disgraceful!"

"She came home because she had nowhere else to go?" Agnes asked, her face pinched with sorrow. "We should have forgiven her, Bedelia. It was a very long time ago."

"Bedelia does not forgive," Grandmama answered Agnes. "Not that there was anything of Maude's that needed pardon. Tragically there are some people who can never forgive a gift, especially from someone who is aware of their vulnerability. Sometimes it is harder to forgive a gift than an injury, because you have incurred a debt, and in your own eyes you have lost control, and your superiority."

There was an electric silence.

"Those who themselves do not forgive find it impossible to believe that others do," Grandmama went on. "So they expect vengeance where there is none, and strike out to defend themselves from a blow that existed only in their own guilty imaginations."

Arthur leaned forward. "I think you had better stop speaking in riddles, Mrs. Ellison. I have very little idea of what you are talking about . . ."

"Neither has she!" Bedelia said tartly. "Really Arthur, you should have more sense than to encourage her. Can't you see that she has been drinking? Let us speak of something civilized and stop descending into personal remarks. It is extremely vulgar." She spoke as if that was the end of the matter.

Arthur drew in his breath, but it was Agnes who answered. She looked at Grandmama directly. "Was Maude ill? Did she know she was going to die, and that was why she came home at last? To make peace?"

"No," Grandmama replied with authority. "As I said, there was nothing to keep her in Persia anymore, nor was it safe."

"She had made enemies, no doubt," Bedelia observed. "You did not say that this man was married to someone else, but knowing Maude, I have no doubt that it was true."

"Oh, Bedelia, you should forgive her

that!" Agnes pleaded. "It was forty years ago! And she is gone now. It's Christmas!"

"Don't be so feeble!" Bedelia accused her. "Wrong does not suddenly become right just because of the season."

Agnes blushed scarlet.

"Of course it doesn't," Grandmama agreed vehemently. "Some debts can be forgiven, but there are some that have to be paid, one way or another."

"I don't care for your opinion, Mrs. Ellison," Bedelia said frigidly.

"There is no reason why you should," again Grandmama agreed with her. "But you care about your family's opinions. In the end it is really all you have. That, and the knowledge within yourself, of course. Perhaps that is why Maude was happy, in the deepest sense. She knew she was loved, and no matter what the cost, she had done the right thing."

"I have no idea what you are talking about!"

"Yes you do. You are probably the only one who does." Nothing was going to stop Grandmama. "When you were a young woman, and even more beautiful than you are now, Mrs. Harcourt," — she glanced at Zachary — "he fell in love with you. And like many young people, you did not deny yourselves the pleasure of love."

Bedelia hissed in her breath, but the shame in Zachary's face made her denial impossible.

"But then Mr. Harcourt came along, and he was a far better catch, so you went after him instead," Grandmama continued relentlessly. "And you caught him, at least his admiration for your beauty, and a certain physical appetite. You also did not deny yourselves. After all, you fully intended to marry him. Which would all have gone very well, had not Maude returned home, and Mr. Harcourt fell truly in love with her."

Bedelia's eyes on her were like daggers.

Grandmama ignored them, but her heart was pounding almost in her throat. If she were wrong, catastrophically, insanely wrong, she would be ruined forever. Her mouth was dry, her voice rasping. "You were furious that Maude, of all people, should take your lover, but there was worse to fol-low. You learned that you were with child. Mr. Sullivan's of course. But it could have been Mr. Harcourt's, for all he knew. That gave you your perfect weapon for regaining everything. You told him. Being a man of honor, in spite of his lapse of self-control, he broke off his relationship with Maude, whom he truly loved, as she loved him, and he married you. He paid a bitter price for his self-indulgence. So did your sister, rather than allow you to be shamed."

There were gasps of breath, the clink of cutlery, even a broken glass stem. "That is what you cannot forgive — that you wronged her," she went on regardless. "And she sacrificed her happiness for yours — and perhaps for Mr. Harcourt's honor. Although I believe it was actually Mr. Sullivan's, in fact."

Arthur stared at Bedelia, a stunned and terrible look in his eyes. "Randolph is not mine, and you know it," he said very quietly.

"Are . . . are you sure?" Agnes asked. Then she looked more closely at Bedelia, and did not ask again.

"What does she mean that you could not forgive?" Arthur asked Bedelia.

"I have no idea!" Bedelia replied. "She is an inquisitive, meddling old woman who listens at doors and hears half stories, gossips with other old women who should know better, and apparently listened to Maude's self-delusions of her own romantic youth."

"It wasn't a delusion," Arthur told her very quietly. "I loved Maude as I have never loved anyone else in my life, before or since. But I could not marry her because you told me that you were carrying my child. I can't blame you for that, it was my doing as much as yours. Nor can I blame Zachary. He was no worse than I, and by heaven you were beautiful. But Maude was funny and kind. She was brave and warm and honest, and she was generous with life, with her own spirit. Her beauty would have lasted forever, and grown with time rather than fade. I knew it then, and I was proved right when she came back, even after forty years, which were like a lifetime while she was gone, and nothing at all once she returned."

"Oh, Arthur!" Agnes breathed out. "How terrible for you."

Zachary was looking at Agnes with amazement.

"I found the rest of the peppermint water," Grandmama said in the silence.

"I beg your pardon?" Arthur frowned.

Grandmama wavered for an instant. Should she tell them, or was this enough? But would it last? There would be no further chance. She turned to Bedelia and saw the fury in her eyes.

"You told Maude when you gave her the macadamia nuts, which are so indigestible to some of us, that you had very little peppermint water, just the end of one bottle, sufficient for a single dose. But actually you

163

had plenty. There is some in my room, and some in the other guest rooms also. A nice courtesy, especially over a festive season when we will all eat a little heavily."

"What has that to do with anything at all?" Clara demanded. "Why are we talking about peppermint water? Are you quite mad?"

"I wish I were," Grandmama answered. "It would be so much less ugly an answer than the truth. I don't eat macadamia nuts myself. They give me indigestion . . ."

Zachary was staring at her as if he could not believe his ears.

Agnes looked appalled.

"But peppermint water would help," Grandmama carried on. "Unless of course, it were laced with foxglove leaves. Then it would kill. Most of us who have ever arranged flowers know that. There are a few one must be careful of, especially with children about: laburnum, monk's hood, belladonna, and of course foxgloves. Such handsome flowers, but the distilled juice can cause the heart to fail. It is used in medicine to slow it down if it is racing, but only a very little, naturally."

"That is a wicked thing to suggest!" Clara was horrified. "How . . . how dare you?"

Randolph touched her gently. "There is no need to be afraid, my dear. She could not possibly prove it." He gulped. "Could you?"

Grandmama looked at him and realized it was a question. "I don't know," she replied. "I had not considered trying to, although it might not be too difficult. I don't think that is what matters. It is knowing the truth that is important. It gives you the freedom to do whatever you choose to, knowing right from wrong." She turned to Arthur, waiting for him to speak.

But he was not looking at her. His gaze did not move from Bedelia's face, and he read in it the fear and the hatred that betrayed her. Whatever she had said, he would know what she had done.

Randolph was staring at his mother with horror and pity in his face, and a revulsion he could not hide. He turned swiftly to Zachary, then embarrassed, away again. Zachary was looking at him with wonder, and an intensity quite naked in his eyes.

Arthur sighed. He spoke to Grandmama as if Bedelia had ceased to exist. "You mentioned a garden in Persia that Maude described to you as if she loved it. Have you any idea where it was, exactly?"

"No, but I believe Mrs. Dowson would know," Grandmama replied. "Maude wrote to her quite regularly. I imagine she would be happy to tell you."

"Good. I have a great desire to see it, since she loved it so much. You made it sound marvelous also, Mrs. Ellison, and for that I shall always be grateful to you. The truth you have shown us is terrible, but deep as it cuts, a clean wound will heal, in time."

"You . . . you can't go to Persia now, Papa . . . I mean . . . ," Randolph faltered and stopped.

Arthur smiled at him, gently and with great affection. "You will always be my son in spirit, Randolph, and I will always love you as such. But I can go to Persia and I will. I shall write to Lord Woollard and decline a peerage. I may return from Persia one day, and I may not. The estate will provide for your mother. Please see that Mrs. Ellison is safely returned to St. Mary in the Marsh tomorrow. Now I shall wish you good night." He rose to his feet. He was still a startlingly handsome man, but it was his dignity that remained in the mind. "And good-bye," he added, before turning and leaving the room without looking behind him. He did not once glance at Bedelia.

Zachary reached out his hand to Agnes, and very slowly, as if uncertain that it could be true, she took it.

Reluctantly Grandmama abandoned her dinner and excused herself also. It was quite impossible to remain. She had shown them the truth. What they did with it she should not influence, only hope.

Upstairs in her bedroom she sank down into the chair. Suddenly her legs were weak and she found she was trembling. Had she done enough? Should she have tried harder to prove something that would stand the test of trial and the law?

As it was now, the family knew the truth. There could be no denying that. Arthur would leave, perhaps forever. Bedelia would probably never see him again. People would know, in the way that they do. They would look at her and whisper. There would be speculation, most of it ugly. The kindest she would receive would be pity, and that would be the most painful of all to a woman like Bedelia. She would see it in their glances in the street, the half-hidden smiles.

Gradually perhaps even some of the truth would emerge, but imagination would be more colorful, and crueler. Agnes and Zachary would be happy with each other at last, and perhaps with Randolph too, and Clara. Old Mrs. Dowson would understand a great deal. She might be discreet, but Bedelia would know that she knew, and would never allow Maude's name to be blackened.

Bedelia would be provided for, waited on, but starved of friendship or admiration. No one would care how beautiful she had been, or how clever. She would be alone, a woman unloved.

At a glance, that was a gentler punishment than trial, and possibly the gallows, or possibly a verdict of innocence. But it would be more certain, and far, far longer. She would taste it for the rest of her life.

But the others would be happy, perhaps for the first time in their lives.

Grandmama stopped shaking and sat still, slowly beginning to smile, even if there was sadness in it, and pity.

In the morning Zachary drove her back through the deepening snow to St. Mary in the Marsh. He did not speak much, but she felt a great certainty that he had at last realized that Agnes was not a paler, second-best version of Bedelia, but a kinder if less brave person, a gentler, more generous one, who might now, at last, find the courage to be the best. And she had always truly loved him.

"Thank you, Mrs. Ellison," he said as the trap rounded the last corner through the dazzling snow and she saw Joshua and

Caroline's house blazing with lights.

"I hope you will be happy," she replied, meaning it far more than the simple words could convey.

"I . . . I understand why you and Maude were such good friends," he said earnestly. "Even in so short a time. You are like her. You have such courage to tell the truth, however difficult, and such joy for life. I am amazed at your compassion for even the weakest of us. I imagine you will have a wonderful Christmas, because you will make it so. But I wish it for you just the same."

"I will," she assured him as they drew up in front of the door. It opened and Joshua came down the step and across the grass to the trap to assist her. "I shall have the best Christmas of my life," she went on, still speaking to Zachary. "I am beginning to understand what it truly means."

"Welcome home, Mama-in-law," Joshua said with surprise lifting his eyebrows. He gave her his arm and she alighted.

"Thank you, Joshua." She smiled at him. "Happy Christmas, my dear. I have wonderful things to tell you, brave and beautiful things, when I can think how to find words for them. About hope and honor, and what love really means. Your aunt Maude was a very wonderful woman. She has given me the greatest gift of all — an understanding of Christmas itself."

"Yes, I see that," Joshua said with sudden conviction. "It is perfectly plain. Happy Christmas, Mama-in-law."

ABOUT THE AUTHOR

Anne Perry is the bestselling author of *No Graves As Yet, Shoulder the Sky,* and *Angels in the Gloom;* two earlier holiday novels, *A Christmas Journey* and *A Christmas Visitor;* and two acclaimed series set in Victorian England. Her most recent William Monk novels are *Death of a Stranger* and *The Shifting Tide.* The popular novels featuring Charlotte and Thomas Pitt include *Southampton Row, Seven Dials,* and *Long Spoon Lane.* Her short story "Heroes" won an Edgar Award. Anne Perry lives in Scotland. Visit her website at www.anneperry. net.

The employees of Thorndike Press hope you have enjoyed this Large Print book. All our Thorndike and Wheeler Large Print titles are designed for easy reading, and all our books are made to last. Other Thorndike Press Large Print books are available at your library, through selected bookstores, or directly from us.

For information about titles, please call:

(800) 223-1244

or visit our Web site at:

www.gale.com/thorndike
www.gale.com/wheeler

To share your comments, please write:

Publisher
Thorndike Press
295 Kennedy Memorial Drive
Waterville, ME 04901